WICKED IS HER SMILE

SCHOOL OF NECESSARY MAGIC BOOK FIVE

JUDITH BERENS   MARTHA CARR   MICHAEL ANDERLE

WICKED IS HER SMILE TEAM

Thanks to the JIT Readers

Daniel Weigert
Mary Morris
James Caplan
Peter Manis
Keith Verret
Tim Bischoff
Larry Omans
Paul Westman
Micky Cocker
John Ashmore

If we've missed anyone, please let us know!

Editor - Lynne Stiegler

From Martha

To everyone who still believes in magic
and all the possibilities that holds.
To all the readers who make this
entire ride so much fun.
And to my son, Louie and so many wonderful friends who
remind me all the time of what
really matters and how wonderful
life can be in any given moment.

From Michael

To Family, Friends and
Those Who Love
To Read.
May We All Enjoy Grace
To Live The Life We Are
Called.

Alison sat comfortably on the train with her new Kindle braille reader on her lap. Soon enough, the special glasses from Shay would be ready. The gnome had assured Shay they would be in Alison's hands by Christmas. He had reassured them more than once, something this special takes time. "Sight for the Drow," he had said. "No small feat."

She had made Shay tell her every detail of her meetings with the gnome, anxiously awaiting the glasses. Sight for the Drow.

She smiled at the thought.

I'll be able to see. The gnome had assured Shay that Alison would be close to normal sight but until she was wearing them, it was impossible to know exactly. Every magical being mixed with an artifact reacted differently. *But soon...*

She ran her fingers over the screen as it moved and formed the words with each page turn. The train ride from home back to school wouldn't take her that long, but she had been engrossed in a new series about trolls and witches that she had found over summer break.

She finished the last chapter of the book, smiled, and let out a deep breath. *Magic is real, and it's returning.*

"Next stop, Denver, Colorado," the announcer called over the speaker as the train pulled up to the station with a whoosh and a spray of steam.

Alison could sense the energies of the people standing on the platform outside her window. She always liked to energy-watch. It was her version of people-watching. There were so many people on the platform going about their day. The sea of energy parted, and she sensed a large group with a deep well of dark magic flowing throughout them.

There was something not right about it—she could feel it in her bones. For a moment, she wasn't sure whether to just let it go or get out and see exactly what they were up to. Fortunately, and unfortunately, with the power she had inside her, she couldn't just let it pass. She grabbed her bag from the seat next to her and dropped her braille reader inside, threw her backpack on, grabbed her suitcase from the overhead, and headed out of the train.

She slung the strap of her suitcase over her chest, making it easier for her to work her way through the crowd. The doors closed behind her and she paused as the train whooshed off, almost rethinking her choice. Alison stepped closer to the group and closed her eyes, allowing her other senses to take over.

"They'll never even see us coming," whispered a witch.

"Exactly. It's perfect," the wizard across from her said, checking to make sure no one else was listening.

Alison waited for them to make a move. When they did, she opened her eyes to sense where they were going. Allowing them to get a bit ahead of her, she followed them up the stairs, into the Starbucks, and out onto the streets of Denver. Her continuing work with Shay to heighten her senses was paying off, allowing her to navigate easily down the street.

The group moved slowly, and Alison kept about a half-block behind them. All the while, she studied their energy and the dark magic swirling around inside them. Her chest got heavy when she recognized that the darkness was similar to what she had seen in her biological father several years before—evil and murderous, with cowardice to it. It almost made her sick to her stomach to think about.

"You should have seen the face of that elf I cornered two days ago." One of the wizards chuckled. "He didn't know whether to run, use his powers, or crap himself."

"Nice." Another laughed. "Those Light scum think they can walk around all high and mighty until you have one cornered."

"Enough. Not out here," the other wizard growled.

Alison swung her bookbag off her shoulders, flipped it around in front of her, and pulled out the bracelet that Shay had given her. Pretty and useful in a fight—the perfect gift.

Shay had gotten it from the same gnome and had been working with Alison on using it all summer. The bracelet was special, and not just anyone could wear it. It was meant for a Drow.

She quickly learned that the artifact refined her abilities. It enhanced the colors of energy and helped her to focus on those energies—light and dark—without getting overwhelmed or confused. It was a temporary replacement till the glasses were ready.

All summer she had worn it as much as she possibly could, but there were two things about the bracelet that disappointed her. First, she could only wear it for so long before its energy gave her a splitting headache, and second, it only held so much energy.

Shay had promised her that they would work on figuring out how to get the artifact to hold more energy, or at least fix the migraines.

Alison put the bracelet on and scanned the energy that ran through them. *Not from this world. Maybe Oriceran.* The dark wizards approached a building, and Alison waited as they walked through the doors before hurrying over and crouching next to a cracked window, where she listened to the group's conversation. They were in there with some normie thugs.

"It took you long enough," one of the thugs growled.

"Don't forget who you're talking to," a wizard barked.

"Sorry," he grumbled, looking down at the floor. "We're just nervous with everything going on."

"I'm sure you are, but we are about to take care of that," the wizard replied, scraping his long nail down the norm's cheek. "Now, is everything set up? I don't want to get there and end up looking like a fool in front of one of the families. This should be an in-and-out: poison the shifters and leave them to the destruction. There're going to be at least five thousand people at that concert, and the band made up of shifters. The crowd won't even know it's not part of the show until they start ripping out throats."

"Why the shifters? Didn't you guys fail miserably when you tried to make them your puppets?"

The wizard flicked his wand at the thug, sending a shower of sparks down the oversized man's front. He yowled and slapped his belly to extinguish them.

The wizard smiled slyly as he enjoyed the brief show. "They aren't the same as magical people. We…" He proudly tapped his chest. "*We* are harder to manipulate and less predictable. Shifters at their roots are dumb animals, like oversized dogs with fangs. They can be trained with a few treats or a really good spell."

The large man scowled at the wizard, still smarting. "It's all taken care of. When you get there, go to the VIP section. Speak to the guard at the door, and let him know Iman sent you."

"Excellent. This cannot fail. We need this push, and I'm tired of our failure rate. We need to make some fucking progress."

Alison took a deep breath and turned from the window, pressing her back against the wall. She couldn't let this happen. They were going to put not only shifters in danger but humans as well. Alison clenched her fists and nodded, knowing she had to do something about it. She could feel the energy pulsing through her almost as if her magic knew it was time to fight.

She put her bags down on the sidewalk and took in a deep breath, then kicked the door open. It banged against the wall as Alison marched into the open space. She could sense the energy of the dark witches and wizards, and the energies surrounding the norms. One of the thugs chuckled and put his hands on his hips while the wizards pulled their wands out of habit.

"Well, well, well. Look what we have here—some little girl. What are you doing, little girl? You come to save the day?" He laughed loudly until one of the wizards hit him in the chest.

"She's no little girl. She's a Drow!"

Immediately the wizards twisted their wands upward, and Alison threw her arms out to the side and sent out a dark blanket over them. She could still sense their energies, but they couldn't see her. They stumbled about as they waited for the darkness to lift and she let her magic fly, sending out beams of light that struck the thugs and wrapped them up. By the time the darkness lifted, only dark wizards were standing, and they looked in amazement at the humans piled in the corner.

"We will not let some young Drow make a fool of us!" The leader of the group was furious and slashed his wand through the air, sending multiple dark arrows soaring toward Alison.

She sensed the dark magic and jumped to the side as the arrows flew by her, then lifted her hand up and blew across her palm. Bits of sparkling blue magic cascaded from her lips and over her fingertips and shot toward the wizards. They sparkled and shimmered around the dark wizards like fairies, glowing so brightly that the wizards were temporarily blinded.

Alison would make sure they weren't going to do any damage to the shifters or anyone else.

"You think you can come to my world and harm my people? Think again."

She lifted her arms, and with a downward swish sent out a bolt of energy that blew the wizards into the wall behind them, then kicked their dropped wands across the room. She clapped her hands together, moving all the wizards into a large group.

She used her magic to control the leader's movements. With no control of his own, he walked toward her. His eyes were wide, and he was unable to speak.

"Pick up that rope," Alison commanded, knowing that he couldn't resist. "Now, tie yourself up with the others."

The wizard did as he was told and tied them together.

"All of you, hold out your arms and push up the sleeves of your robes," she commanded, backing it up with a spray of stinging sparks. "Lift up your arms, higher."

They did as they were told and pulled up their sleeves, revealing the underside of their arms. Alison's eyes glowed, and her silver hair shimmered as she swiped her hand right and left, branding each wizard with a skull and roses. When she was done, she snapped their wands in half, throwing the pieces in different directions.

She turned back as she was leaving.

"Leave the shifters alone, or I'll find my way back here just to deal with you. The next time I'll leave an even stronger impression."

She knew it wasn't exactly what Brownstone would have done. Her father would have made sure they couldn't get up again, permanently. But Alison still wanted to believe the darkness could be held back. Only time would tell.

Alison walked out of the building with a smile on her

face, running her fingers over the braille watch that Brownstone had given her at the beginning of summer.

"Damn!"

She realized there was only one more train she could take back to school. She grabbed her bags and moved toward the oncoming energy, through the back wall of the Starbucks, and down the staircases, onto the platform just as the train arrived. When she found a seat, she put her bags in her lap and tried to catch her breath.

She was once again just an ordinary student trying to get to school on time, only now she had a secret.

2

Alison bounced up and down on her seat as the jitney drove down the winding country road to the entrance of the old converted mansion. The gates were open for the jitney this year, instead of making it stop in front of the gates. Alison saw the magical energy from the two wizards at their post on either side of the gate.

As the bus moved through, Alison could sense a heightened pulse of energy from the protective spells across the opening to repel anyone who should not be there. The bus came to a stop and Mrs. Beasley, pushed on the stubborn black handle, letting out a familiar grunt.

Alison gathered her things, walking behind everyone else as they exited.

"Have a good year," the bus driver called in a kindly tone.

"Thank you. You as well." Alison hesitated, waiting for everyone else to get off.

"Was there something else, dear?" asked Mrs. Beasley, the usual driver.

"Were those guards in front of the gates?"

Mrs. Beasley tsked and said, "Oh my, well…" but Alison waited her out. She was always the best source of gossip in all of Albemarle County. Everyone talked to her and she shared tidbits of everything she heard.

"Word, is," she whispered conspiratorially, "the security has been beefed up around the school. Ms. Mara went down into the kemana and hired a couple of beefy kilomeas and glamoured them to look less hairy. Not sure what they can do against dark magic." Mrs. Beasley let out a shiver. "My sister in Minneapolis once tangled with a witch who liked to play in the dark arts. Was not pretty."

"Two Kilomeas is all it takes?" Alison could see Mrs. Beasley's energy warming to a rosy pink. She was excited to share what she knew.

"I didn't see it all myself, mind you. But I hear, there's a few more working the grounds and there's a few traps laid just around the fence. The school's not allowed to lay down traps beyond the property line. There was a big meeting!" Mrs. Beasley reached out, grabbing Alison's arm, giving her a squeeze.

"A meeting in town?"

"Oh yes, dear. There's been an agreement since the school was started that no magic can be laid down outside of the property. Ms. Mara was arguing that these are different times and the children and the school need to be protected. I agree with her but others felt it set a bad precedent and after what happened with the toombic, and then the shifters…" Her voice trailed off.

Alison felt a cold chill despite the season. "Someone suggested the school should close."

Mrs. Beasley let go of Alison's arm. "Only loud Mr. Fenderle. That old fart of an elf, pardon my language. He's always complaining about something. Well, maybe a couple of others, but that was it. Cross my heart." Mrs. Beasley drew a line across her heart. "Oh, you can't see me doing it. Foolish me," she said, flustered. "Well, I swear! I promise!"

Alison thought about what she had seen in the train station. Maybe her father did know best.

"Thank you, Mrs. Beasley, I should go."

"I hope I didn't upset you, dear. Here, let me give you a hug." The bus driver squeezed out of her seat and wrapped Alison in her arms.

"Not at all. It's good to know the school is doing something. Maybe we can help the town get to know us better."

"Now that's a good idea!" chirped the driver, as Alison made her way off the bus.

"Alison!" Izzie yelled, running down the stairs and across the courtyard to greet Alison.

Students were arriving at different points across campus. Some had taken the bus, some came through portals, and others were being dropped off by their parents. It was the first day of Alison's junior year, and she was really glad to be back at school. There were new students, mostly freshmen, and a ton of students from the year before. Alison was glad to see it. She hadn't been sure how many would return, and had imagined walking onto the grounds and only seeing one or two energies.

Alison stopped and watched Izzie's energy move toward her. She glanced behind Izzie to find Kathleen, Emma, and Aya heading her way as well. A big smile moved across Alison's lips. She was ecstatic to see her friends. As Izzie approached, she threw her arms around Alison and hugged her tightly, taking her suitcase from her.

"It's so good to see you! We've been waiting all day for you to get here. We actually thought you would be here about an hour ago," Izzie burbled cheerfully. "It's been too long!"

"You saw me this summer!"

Izzie laughed, "And the stories we have to tell. What took you so long?"

Alison cleared her throat nonchalantly. "Uh, yeah. I had to switch trains. I didn't realize that there was a different one coming in this direction, so I got off in Denver and had to wait. It was pretty busy there."

"That sucks," Kathleen replied with a smile. "I went to Denver once. That was pretty much enough for me. Don't get me wrong, I love Colorado and the skiing, but all I saw in Denver was dirty city and mud. At least you didn't have to stay there long. I was in Denver for a week with my father while he attended some conference. I begged my mom to open a portal, but she refused."

Alison giggled and shrugged. "I didn't really see anything but the platform, and to me, they all look the same."

Kathleen chuckled and gave her a hug, then stepped to the side so Aya and Emma could hug her as well. Emma squeezed her tightly and pulled back, looking at Alison's bright hair.

"I swear, every time I see you, it's like the silver in your hair gets brighter. Maybe it's because it's taken at this point? I love it. I know you can't see it, but it's freaking *awesome*."

Alison laughed and ran her fingers through her hair, swishing it back and forth. "What can I say? Drow is in right now."

All the girls giggled as Aya squeezed Alison's hand, and they started to walk toward the mansion.

"I know late August is hot, but it seriously feels like it's about a thousand degrees out here today. And on top of that, the cicadas are driving me nuts. Let's get inside where it's nice and cool...and quiet."

Inside the mansion, they dropped their bags out of the way and stood in the foyer while they looked at all the students. Coming down the stairs were Luke, Ethan, and Peter, who waved hello. Ethan walked over to Alison and nudged her.

"Hey, there. You excited to be a junior?" He chuckled sarcastically.

"I guess so, if it means you're gonna pull some special junior year April Fools' Day joke."

Kathleen sighed and rolled her eyes. "Don't encourage him."

"I know I've seen you guys like a million times, since we've been video chatting like every day this summer, but I still feel like I haven't seen you forever." Izzie walked up next to Luke and grasped his hand.

"I know, and I just saw you like a month ago," Alison replied thinking about her summer visit with Izzie. "It's just good to be back. I'm glad we're all together again."

"It does suck, though. There are a lot of people here, sure, but a ton didn't come back after what happened with the shifters last year. People just don't seem to understand that it wasn't the shifters' fault." Izzie gripped Luke's hand tighter and smiled up at him.

He smiled back. The two of them turned when they heard the conversation a small group of witches was having as they walked by with their children.

"This school has a serious discipline problem. These kids are just running around like nothing ever happened," said a witch as she pressed her daughter to walk on ahead, shaking her head.

Another witch in large red sunglasses nodded, scowling. "Not to mention, they're letting in half-breeds, barely magicals and worse of all, shifters." The witch shook her head. "It's like they didn't learn last year that shifters can't be trusted. We knew it two decades ago when shifters were erupting all over the place."

"Humans with fur and teeth," hissed a witch, momentarily lifting her foot to look on the bottom of her shoe. "The beasts can't control themselves, yet the school thinks it's okay to just let them run wild in the student body. They'll learn their lesson when some unsuspecting student gets mauled in the hallway."

"They've added security, but is it enough?"

"That's not for the shifters." A mother with long dark hair neatly pulled back in a tortoise shell clip patted the scarf tied around her neck. "Everyone wants to point the finger at the old wizarding families. I don't believe it," she sniffed.

"We send our own children here," hissed a short witch with curly brown hair, and an oversized leather purse slung across her shoulder. "Hell, we could let them in the front gate ourselves if we were that stupid!"

"It's idiots who've gotten their hands on a few complicated spells causing trouble and distracting the school."

"We would never…"

"The council of families has better things to do. The witch in large sunglasses scoffed and shook her head. "Yeah, and if the shifters lose it, we know exactly who they're going to go after first…one of our children."

"If this wasn't the best education in witchcraft on this side of the ocean I'd pull Amy out in a second."

"I made sure Craig learned a few defensive spells over the summer, just in case. I told him he has to look out for himself. Fur and teeth, barely magical," the witch muttered.

Luke easily overheard everything. It wasn't like they were trying to keep it to themselves. His eyes changed to the amber color of his wolf, and he growled in their direction. Izzie covered her mouth and giggled when the witches glared at them. A witch gasped and shook her head, walking faster to catch up and grab her daughter's hand as they all moved farther into the mansion. Izzie turned and gently slapped Luke in the stomach.

"You know you shouldn't do that. The headmistress will have you in detention with Librarian Decker even after you've graduated," she said laughing.

"Yeah? Well, maybe she should remind the bitches posing as witches that they started this twenty years ago. *Then* teach them all a little understanding."

Izzie smiled, wrapped her arms around him, and squeezed tightly, taking a deep breath of his scent. She had been away from him for too long and, feisty or not, she was really glad to be back with him. He was right, though. The war between the shifters and the dark families needed to be over, especially if they were going to attend school together, not to mention integrate within the magical community and with the norms. That was the whole point of this. They were trying to find common ground between all magical beings so they could move forward into the future without situations like what had happened the year before.

"Okay," Kathleen began excitedly. "Boys, we're going to have to leave you for now. We have something to show Alison!"

Alison lifted an eyebrow and squinted, sensing Kathleen's excitement in her energy. "Please don't tell me it's another egg…"

"Don't be silly. I think I learned my lesson on that one the first time." Kathleen laughed. "Did you forget?"

"Forget what?"

Emma clapped her hands and grasped Alison's wrist. "We are juniors now! And though that *does* mean more work, harder classes, and more pressure, it also means we get a new room!"

Slowly a smile moved over Alison's face and she nodded, letting Emma pull her toward the stairwell. The girls were extremely excited to lead Alison to their new room. Upperclassmen got bigger suites. They headed up to the third floor and took a right toward the common area. Alison could sense the energy that floated around the room. Izzie smiled, looking at all the new furniture, the bigger fireplace, and the huge flat screen TV mounted on the wall. At the third door on the left, Kathleen stood to the side with her arm out.

"Ta-da!" she caroled as the girls led Alison into the room.

It was huge, with three four-poster beds against two of the walls. There were wardrobes and dressers for each of them, and beautiful flowered drapes hung from the windows. The floors were lush carpet instead of the tile their previous room had had, and the walls were decorated with moving magical pictures of the scenery of Charlottesville.

Izzie stared at one of the pictures and turned back to the girls. "These pictures change! Earlier today they were pictures of Ruby Falls in springtime. This one's of the mansion's grounds, but it looks like it was taken before the school started."

The bed closest to the doors hadn't been made yet, and Emma looked at it, tightly grasping a post. "There are only five of us. Who's the sixth bed for?"

Everyone shrugged, and Alison walked to the back of the room. She took the bed in the same place that she'd been in the other room and put her backpack on top of the lush feather quilt, turned around and fell backward into the soft bed. For a moment, she just took in the quiet.

From the room next door, Scarlett was barking orders at her cronies right and left. They were seniors now and shared the same dorm as Izzie, Alison, and the other juniors.

"Okay, girls," Scarlett said as she entered the room. "It looks like you've all gotten settled in, so I think it's time we go over the dorm room rules and tell you what lines not to cross."

Alison sat up and turned toward Scarlett's usual uncomfortable energy. Behind her stood some of her friends, looking a little less full of themselves than usual. Scarlett sashayed to the center of the room and looked around, lifting one eyebrow.

"Well, I guess you got one of the cheaper rooms since you don't have a fridge like I do. Anyway, here are a few rules for you. If you can keep it together, we won't have any problems. No one, and I mean *no one*, sets foot in my room. If you need me, you knock and let one of my people know. Every Tuesday, my group and I have the common room to ourselves."

"For what?" Aya asked.

"None of your business," Scarlett snapped. "Also, the seniors use the showers first in the morning, so unless you want to take a shower at four in the morning, wait until we're done."

Scarlett sauntered back over to the door, her people leaving before her. She stopped and turned back as she grabbed the door handle.

"I'll let you know if any new rules come up. Have fun with your new roomie," she said with a giggle.

She slammed the door, making everyone jump. Aya shook her head and turned to the group. "She is just begging for a good practical joke or two."

3

The girls hung their clothes in their new wardrobes and filled their dressers, then organized all their trinkets and school items on the extra shelves at the back of the room. When they were finished, they stowed their suitcases underneath their beds and looked at each other. Emma sat on the edge of her bed, kicking her legs and watching the pictures change on the wall. When the scene changed from the front of the mansion to an aerial shot of the forest nearby, it gave Emma an idea.

"I got it. I think it's time we go find Dorvu. Don't you think?"

Izzie clapped her hands and nodded. "Yes! He's missed everyone so much this summer. I visited him as much as I could, but since I was the only student here, it raised suspicions when I disappeared."

Alison walked forward. "Yeah, and when I came to visit he was nowhere to be found. I want to see how big he's grown."

Kathleen sighed and shrugged. "I suppose we should

visit him. We are his family, after all. But I'm telling you right now, if a bug lands on me I'm sprinting back to the mansion so fast you won't even see me leave."

The girls laughed as they pulled on their shoes and headed out the room. Emma put her arm around Kathleen and they took up the rear, laughing about a plot to make sure none of the bugs touched her. They headed out to the courtyard, then nonchalantly made their way over to the field. They were curious as to how big the dragon had gotten.

As they crossed the fields that overlooked the busy barn and the back end of the garden area, they gazed at the shadowy part of the woods. Emma stopped in her tracks and pointed toward the top of the trees.

"Hey, there he is!"

The girls watched as Dorvu sailed from branch to branch. It was obvious he still couldn't quite fly, at least not out in the open, but he was doing his best to use his wings and practice for when he was strong enough. Izzie glanced back at the courtyard and saw several of the parents look up, then shake their heads. Professor Hudson stopped briefly while showing several of the new students around the property and Izzie lifted an eyebrow, fearful at first that she was going to be angry. Apparently, she knew about Dorvu though, since the look on her face showed admiration as the silver dragon's wings caught the sunlight and reflected it over the trees.

"Well, at least we don't have to worry about Dorvu with Professor Hudson."

Emma got closer to Izzie. "Maybe not, but at the same time, I wouldn't flaunt that we're visiting him. I'm not exactly sure if they know we're the people who brought him here in the first place are. She might very well think it's something that the headmistress did, maybe as something for the new year. I don't want to be around when she figures out the truth."

Izzie nodded, but really she wished things were different. The creatures from Oriceran were amazing. In Izzie's opinion, things like magical dragons, shifters, and even the faeries that frequented the forest were exactly what she thought they would need in the future when magic became more prevalent on Earth. She could picture the humans being dazzled by the beauty of these creatures, and that could help humans be more comfortable when magic was used in front of them. At the same time, though, she could also see how Dorvu could've easily turned out to be a bad idea, and the last thing magicals needed were more bad ideas.

Once the girls reached the barn, they crossed back over the campus. They were afraid that they'd accidentally lead someone to Dorvu, and they couldn't have that happen. Alison glanced toward Horace's workshop, hoping she would sense Horace, but he wasn't there.

The girls quickly moved behind the workshop and waited a moment before hurrying into the woods. They maneuvered over the fallen trees and through the remnants of last fall's leaves and headed deeper into the forest. Finally, when they had reached Dorvu's clearing deep in the woods, they stopped.

"I think we're good," Emma said, looking behind them for anyone who might have followed.

Alison nodded. "I don't sense anyone but us."

Izzie cleared her throat and cupped her hands by her mouth. "Dorvu! We're all here to see you! Come visit us!"

"Dorvu!" Alison called. "It's your family. We missed you. Come see us!"

The girls backed up to the tree line when they heard the rustling of leaves and the crackling of branches coming from the distance. When they looked into the canopy, they saw trees swaying closer and closer to them, and Dorvu, his silver scales glistening brightly in the sun, emerged. He flapped his wings a couple times and slowly let himself drop to the ground in front of them, blowing out a blast of wintery air from his nose.

"Whoa." The girls giggled and stumbled back. Their hair was frosted and covered in small ice crystals.

He was bigger than they'd thought he would be at that point. Then again, none of them really knew what to expect. He tilted his head and looked at them happily. A mouse tail hung from his mouth, and he slurped it in and bent forward until he was at eye level with the girls. Everyone but Alison grimaced, even as Dorvu blew cool air on them to relive the hot stickiness of the day.

Emma and Kathleen wrinkled their noses.

"Eau de mouse, ewwww…"

"You've gotten so big!"

"He sure has," Horace said, walking into the clearing behind them.

His dog barked as he walked beside him, happy to see the girls but not so happy to see the dragon. Dorvu snorted, blowing ice crystals all over the dog, who shook his fur to dislodge them. The ice fell to the ground and melted almost instantly. Horace chuckled and patted his dog on the head.

"Welcome back, ladies! I was wondering where you were. I went to the mansion to find you, but you weren't in your rooms, or so Scarlett said."

Alison held out her hand and petted the dog when he ran over to her. She looked up from him and smiled at Horace's comforting energy. "We wanted to see Dorvu. I missed him when I was here visiting. Izzie said it was really hard to find him all summer."

"I've been venturing farther into the woods. I'm getting kind of tired of rabbits and mice," Dorvu said grabbing their attention. "If I had known you were here I would've stuck around, but *somebody* forgot to tell me you were coming."

Dorvu looked at Izzie and shook his head. The coldness of his breath created ice on Izzie's hair. She laughed as she pulled her hair into a ponytail and secured it with a band from her wrist. She hugged the dragon's snout and kissed him on the cheek.

"I'm sorry, Dorvu," she whispered. "I won't forget next time. I promise."

Horace chuckled and shook his head. "So, I heard my brother's daughter—my niece Jennifer—is going to be rooming with you guys this year."

Kathleen nodded. "Oh, so *that's* who the sixth bed is for! That's exciting!"

"I think so. She's kind of nervous, but I told her you girls would make her feel right at home. She's half witch on her mother's side, and she's just learning how to use those powers and make them stronger. Actually, she's back in the barn with the horses. You guys want to meet her?"

All the girls nodded, and Izzie patted Dorvu on the snout. "We'll come visit you later, Dorvu. Maybe we'll bring the new girl. You can welcome her with a breath of fresh, cold air."

"I'll be waiting for your call," Dorvu replied, offering his best dragon smirk.

The girls followed Horace out of the woods and across the field to the barn. When they walked inside, they found a tall, thin girl standing in one of the stalls petting a beautiful chestnut colored stallion quarter horse. She had that trademark family red hair, and large curls that bounced all over her head and down her back. She wore perfectly-shined riding boots over her jeans and looked like she was incredibly comfortable standing right next to the horse.

"Hi," Kathleen said, smiling.

Jennifer turned toward the girls and smiled, then glanced at Horace, who gave a big grin and nodded. "These are the girls you are going to be rooming with, and hopefully making amazing friendships with. This is Kathleen, Emma, Aya, Izzie, and Alison."

Izzie stepped forward and shook Jennifer's hand. "I really like your riding boots. I would love to get some one day since I love being around the horses."

"Really? I love horses. I've been around them my whole life. In fact, I hope that one day I can own a horse farm. At least, that's my goal if I'm not doing something crazy with magic or something."

Horace nodded and winked at her.

"Jennifer here is playing down her horse skills a bit. She's actually a champion rider. She's been riding since she was old enough to walk, and I've been going back to Texas to watch her events whenever I can. Now that we have her here, she can give our horses a good workout."

The girls were incredibly excited to meet Jennifer. She melded right into the group almost instantaneously. Alison watched her beautiful energy bounce around the horses. Streams of excitement, nerves, and curiosity wove around her as she met each of them. In between all of that were flickering waves of mischief, so Alison knew right away that Jennifer would have no trouble fitting in with them.

"No, I haven't gone into the great hall yet," Jennifer replied excitedly. "I came early with Horace, but I felt weird walking around the mansion all by myself. I just stayed out with the horses mostly and helped Horace whenever he needed it."

The girls got to know Jennifer a little bit better as they headed back to the dorm. She was bubbly and happy, and she seemed to fit in well with everyone, both on a group and individual basis. There was something for her to talk about with each of them. She was quick to notice the beautiful dress Kathleen was wearing, which immediately started a conversation about fashion.

"Where I'm from in Texas, people are either extremely country, or they try to keep up with fashion as much as possible. That's where I fall. I like to keep up with fashion, but not the really weird stuff. I like the pieces that are timeless."

Kathleen nodded excitedly. "Yes! I mean, I have some pieces that are *not* timeless, that's definitely true, but the sleek lines you can keep in your closet for ten years and still be fashionable—those are what I love. Elegance with a modern feel, that's what I always tell my mom when we're shopping."

For Emma and Aya, it was her down-home nature and desire to be her own person, but at the same time do things for others. The way she described her family reminded Aya of her own, and that alone was enough to bond the girls almost instantly. Izzie was sold as soon as she saw her with the horses, considering she herself had this way with animals that was just astonishing. For Alison, it was her energy—a mixture of so many different things and none of them bad. Alison knew she would fit right in, and she was really glad to have another person who she could pull into her family.

As they crossed the field into the courtyard, they found Peter, Ethan, and Luke playing hacky sack with some other students. Ethan was using his elf magic to keep the hacky sack aloft when it came to him, which gave him time to kick it to the other player. Half the boys chuckled, and the other half groaned and rolled their eyes.

Luke growled softly, "Dude, I thought we said no magic. When you go off to college, and you're playing this game with the normals, you can't go whipping out your magic just to keep it floating in the air near you."

"Well, when I go to college with the normies, I'll have to figure that out." Ethan chuckled.

"Hey, guys, I want to introduce you to our new room-mate," Kathleen said excitedly as Peter dropped the hacky sack. "This is Jennifer. She's a transfer student. She's a witch, and the niece of our favorite groundskeeper, Horace!"

"Nice to meet you," Luke replied, nodding. "We have an empty bed in our room too. We have no idea who it belongs to, so he must be another late arrival."

Ethan's eyes widened as he stared at Jennifer and shook her hand. "Nice to meet you. You can sit next to me in the hall for the welcome back party. I'll give you the lowdown on everybody there."

Izzie giggled and leaned toward Alison. "Uh-oh, looks like somebody knocked Grace right out of the running."

The girls giggled as they headed inside for welcome back luncheon. Ethan put his hand out as they walked in.

"So, this is the hall or the cafeteria, as we usually call it, unless there's a dance or some crazy event."

"Wow." Jennifer looked at the tall ceilings, beautiful artwork, and rows of tables and chairs.

Some of the parents of the new students tried to follow their kids into the hall, only to find themselves magically back outside again. Their kids giggled, waving to their parents from the doorway. They were more than relieved to have some freedom. The group walked over to their normal table and stood talking to the others while they waited to take a seat.

"Normally, when it's not a luncheon, you come in and then just think about what you want to eat, and it appears on a plate. We always sit here, by the way," Ethan explained to Jennifer.

Jennifer looked around and nodded. "That's cool. I wonder if they'll let me take my meals out at the barn with the horses."

Across the table, Alison stood next to an empty chair, keeping her eyes out for Tanner's telltale energy. She hadn't spotted him since coming back to school. Luke and Izzie stood close together and held hands. They acted as if they hadn't seen each other for years, even though they had gotten together over the summer. For them, there was not enough time in the day to spend with each other. Horace entered the hall with his dog and closed the large door. Professor Hudson walked to the front of the stage, swishing her wand to flicker the lights that magically hovered near the walls to silence the room.

Professor Regency walked past the table and clapped Luke on the shoulder, nodding excitedly. "Luke, it's good to see you back."

"Coach Regency, it's good to see you too, sir."

"I'm really excited about the new Louper season. I think we have a real chance to go all the way this year. We came so close last year. What have you been doing over the summer, Luke? You're definitely one of the best up-and-coming players on the team."

"Thanks, coach. I practiced when ever I had a chance."

Professor Regency gave him a thumbs up. "The season is split in two this year, starting earlier and we have to get the tryouts going. More schools have formed a team so this semester we'll have the first tournament and then an even bigger one next semester. I'm really counting on players like you to pull together. It'll be a long, physical challenge. See you on the field," he said, and headed to the stage.

Luke sat down in the chair next to Izzie and took her hand in his, smiling. "I really do think we can win this year, at least the first tournament." Izzie squeezed his hand.

Headmistress Mara Berens walked up the steps to the front of the stage and touched her throat with a glowing hand, letting the light seep in. She held up her hand to silence the last bit of whispering and smiled.

"Welcome!" her voice roared through the cafeteria. "For you returning students, welcome back. And for all our new students both freshmen and those who have transferred, welcome to the School of Necessary Magic! We are all excited to be back in session, and we look forward to a year that is both educational and enlightening." She held out her hand and let a ball of blue light rise from her palm and change into a bird that circled the room, light trailing behind it as it slowly faded.

The freshmen in the room oohed and aahed, smiles coming to their faces.

The headmistress clapped her hands and looked over at the table where Izzie and her friends were still talking quietly under their breath. They shushed each other and looked at the floor to avoid her glare. She took a deep breath and opened her arms wide to the room.

"Before we begin, lets clear the air about last year. Transparency is healthy for all of us. Others have felt that I shouldn't talk to you about it. We should just let it go, and let it all die down, go away. However, you live here, eat here and sleep here. This is your home for nine months out of the year, and as a family, we can talk about harder things." Mara Berens folded her hands behind her back, gathering her strength.

"Last year, someone poisoned our shifter students. The students were never in any danger from the shifters, but the real truth is the shifters were in danger from everyone else. Luckily, we went through a hard moment but no one was hurt. We are working diligently to find out who did this."

The other professors looked at each other. "I hope she knows what she's doing," whispered Professor Powell.

"It's her choice," said Professor Grant, calmly. "We'll support her, no matter what," she said, leveling her gaze at him.

"I scoured the library for a few new spells to protect the fences but I can't be sure till they're tested."

Professor Grant pressed her eyes shut momentarily. "Let's hope it doesn't come to that. The government heard about it and wanted to pull rank on the school and put up their own set of rules. Mara was able to get them to compromise with all the added security, but if one more thing…" Her voice trailed off.

The headmistress smiled again. "This year is set up to be one of the most exciting yet. We have many special things planned for this year, and it all begins with today's luncheon. Well, that and a mixer tonight after dinner, so everyone can get to know each other better."

Scarlett leaned her head back and let out a groan. The headmistress looked at her with a smirk.

"To start out our luncheon, I would like Scarlett to stand up and wave at everyone." Scarlett instantly changed her attitude and smiled, always the chameleon. She stood up and gave the crowd a pageant wave.

"This is Scarlett, your student body president. If anyone

has concerns or questions, or even ideas about how to make the school year run smoother, Scarlett is the one to go to. She will make sure your ideas and your concerns reach our ears as soon as possible. Now, without further ado, please enjoy your lunch. I look forward to seeing you after dinner tonight at the mixer."

There was a broken round of applause, then a wave of chatter and laughter swept across the room as the students started their luncheon. The food that appeared on the plates varied, depending on what the student was in the mood for. The students carried their plates as they mingled with friends they'd missed all summer. Now that the group had been in school for three years, there were friends—and frenemies, for that matter—around every corner.

The order of things hadn't changed, though. The jocks still sat with the jocks, the artists still with the artists, and the science/magic nerds clustered together in the corner, a puff of smoke coming up from the table. The only group that had a little of everything was Alison's and Izzie's. That didn't, however, mean that they didn't have a ton of friends in the rest of the cafeteria. They walked around, welcoming the others back and chatting with them about their summers.

"What is *that*?" Jennifer asked Izzie, looking at the Louper table.

"The thing floating above the table? Oh, that's the Loupers' coat of arms, the Cardinal!"

Jennifer nodded, and her eyes shifted toward the science table. "And...what exactly are *they* doing?"

Izzie giggled and covered her mouth as she glanced at Peter. "Those are the kids who use science and magic together. Kinda like our friend Peter here, but you'll witness that in the future. Looks like they're trying to build something, although I'm not sure exactly what."

Jennifer lifted an eyebrow and tilted her head to the right. "Whatever it is, there's a fork in the middle of it."

Alison was still unable to find Tanner, but he had shown up late on more than one occasion. Everyone congregated back at the table just as the headmistress walked up and cleared her throat.

"I just wanted to stop by and say hello to everyone. I also wanted to find out how Jennifer was doing."

Jennifer swallowed her green Jell-O and nodded, smiling. "Really well, headmistress. Everyone's been very welcoming, and they have been showing me around the mansion and the grounds."

The headmistress nodded. "Good. Let's make sure that continues. I am a very good friend of Jennifer's Great Aunt Estelle, who lives in Austin."

4

That night after dinner, everyone went up to change clothes for the mixer. The hall's tables and chairs were removed, and the ceiling was enchanted with the night sky, which gave everything a soft glow. Everyone wore semi-formal attire for the mixer—cocktail dresses for the girls, and button-up shirts and dress pants for the guys. The freshmen, however, had no idea what to wear and ended up overdressed in fancy dresses and tuxedos. They all seemed insecure about it, but at least they had each other.

Izzie's group arrived just after the freshmen. Luke and Izzie stood to the side, hand-in-hand, and watched as everyone walked around, and the upperclassmen snickered at the freshmen. Standing beside them, Ethan did small acts of magic to try to impress Jennifer.

"See? It turns into a rose, and you can actually smell it," Ethan said, holding a magical rose in his palm.

"Cool," Jennifer said, not really impressed. "Do you know who loves roses? My horse back at the stables at my parents' house. Her name is Rosalie. I named her that because when she was just a baby, she would head straight for the rosebushes. I don't know how many times I picked thorns out of her poor nose."

Ethan tried to smile and nod, but he was slightly disappointed. He closed his hand, letting the rose dissipate. He bit his bottom lip and looked around for a moment before taking out his wand and creating a tiny pony in his hand. He floated it around her, then brought it back to his palm, where he made it disappear in a puff of smoke.

"That looks just like my other horse…"

When the rest of the group arrived, they moved around the room saying hello to various people, including the professors who were there. They avoided Scarlett, who was pontificating about the burden of leadership.

"It's exhausting, but at the same time so rewarding," Scarlett declaimed with an air of drama.

She acted as if she'd actually done something already when they were only twelve hours into the first day back, and classes hadn't even started yet. Kathleen rolled her eyes and shook her head, then looked at Emma and made a face. Emma giggled and waved at Alison and Izzie across the room. Izzie smiled and waved before turning back to Alison.

"My summer was better than usual," Izzie said, catching up with Alison on the events of the summer. "I got to see you, I got to see Luke, and the headmistress was pretty much off doing her own thing the whole time. I mostly explored the grounds and realized how much stuff is here that I didn't even know about. It's all stuff from before the school was the school. You know, since this mansion has been here for a really long time."

"That's cool." Alison smiled. "You'll have to show me later. How about your dreams? How are those going?"

Izzie sighed and leaned against the wall. "I don't know. Fragments of other memories have come back to me. The problem is, none of them make any sense. Like this one blur of a memory that I keep having over and over. I'm walking down the streets of a city, but it's not a city with super-tall buildings. All the buildings are no more than maybe six or seven stories tall at most. Then I walk out into this huge lawn with two monuments on each side. I have no idea what's going on. I…"

Izzie stopped talking, figuring she could tell Alison what she had dreamed later. Instead, she focused her attention on Tanner as he walked through the doors of the hall. She elbowed Alison in the side.

"Someone you've been looking for just walked through the doors."

Alison gazed across the hall toward the doors, where she found Tanner's familiar energy walking through across the floor. She let out a deep breath and felt her heartbeat speed up. She had been waiting all day to see Tanner and was starting to worry that something had happened to him. His energy was as comforting as it always had been, only this time, there were streams of excitement running through it as he walked toward her. His excitement made her happy, and her cheeks got red from knowing that he was looking forward to seeing her. All the fear and nervousness went away, and she couldn't help but remember the amazing conversations they'd had during video chats, texting, and late-night talks when Brownstone and Shay were gone.

"There's the face I've been waiting all day to see," Tanner said, grabbing Alison's hands.

"I thought maybe you decided not to come back this year," Alison joked.

Tanner squeezed her hands and chuckled. "Well, I thought about it, but there's this girl here. I just can't get her off my mind."

"Oh yeah?" Alison giggled. "Anyone I know?"

Tanner pulled her close and hugged her tightly, grateful that they were in each other's arms again. Alison leaned her face against his warm chest and took a deep breath, not wanting to let go. He pulled back and gave her a kiss on the forehead before turning to the rest of the hall.

"Sorry it took me so long," he said with a sigh. "First, I was supposed to get picked up by my caseworker, who was going to bring me to the train station, but that fell through. Then the people I was staying with were supposed to portal me in, but they were both stuck in traffic and couldn't get back to the house in time. So, after about five hours, the headmistress checked in with me because she was worried I wasn't here and ended up bringing me back with her."

"Oh," Alison replied, wrinkling her brow. "I didn't even know the headmistress left."

"I mean, she only kind of left. She opened a portal into my living room and pulled me through." He laughed. "At least she remembered. I was starting to think that I was going to have to hitch a ride using my thumb."

Alison smiled and squeezed his hand. "You're pretty cute. Somebody would've picked you up."

"I don't know. At least I had an eventful summer. I spent the whole time working with other magical orphans. It was pretty cool, and they gave me a new perspective on life."

"Hopefully not *that* new." Alison smiled. "Otherwise, I'll have to reintroduce myself."

Everywhere Izzie looked, she saw students eating, drinking, and generally catching up with each other after a long summer away. It was Izzie's favorite time in the school—the moment where everyone realized how much they missed each other and not just those in her group. The other groups had also created small families in their home away from home. It was a camaraderie that Izzie didn't remember seeing anywhere else in her life. Right in the middle of it, however, the hall doors blew open, catching everyone's attention.

Stepping through was a tall, dark-haired wizard, rolling his suitcase behind him. "Looks like I'm in the right place."

"Here comes trouble," Peter whispered to Ethan.

The guy walked around the cafeteria, shaking everyone's hand and introducing himself. Emma looked at Kathleen and raised an eyebrow, and Kathleen rolled her eyes again. Emma giggled, always entertained by Kathleen's reactions. She was waiting for the day Kathleen was actually surprised, shocked, or excited. Usually, she just got an eye roll or a sigh, which exactly fit Kathleen's personality.

"Name's Jason Parker," he said, shaking Tanner's hand and looking at the others with a nod. "I'm from Chicago."

Luke whispered into Izzie's ear, "Do you know who that is?"

Izzie shook her head.

"He's really rich, and a member of a very old, very well-known dark wizard family. I knew he was coming before we got here this year. My father heard it through the grapevine. Apparently, he's a junior and a transfer from some private magic school in Chicago that finally booted him. I have no idea what for, but probably something to do with dark magic."

Jason looked down at the paper in his hand and back up at the other guys. "Wait, are you Peter, Ethan, Luke, and Tanner?"

Ethan nodded. "That we are."

"Sweet. Looks like I found my new roommates."

The guys talked a little bit more, realizing they probably needed to since he would be rooming with them. Alison studied his energy curiously. It was unlike anything she had seen before. She noticed the dark streak, but there was also playfulness and lightness, and a whole mixture of other things. In fact, given that he was trying to control the conversation and act all big and brooding, there was more to him than he was letting on.

Jason cleared his throat and turned to Alison, immediately putting on the charm. "Hello, there. I don't know how I didn't notice that beautiful silver hair. I'm Jason."

Alison smirked and shook his hand, sensing that he was holding it out. "Alison."

"Well, Alison, in case you haven't noticed, I'm new to the school. Maybe you could show me around."

Tanner immediately took Alison's hand and stood taller

than normal while puffing out his chest. It took everything in Alison's power not to laugh when she saw the streams of jealousy and irritation running through Tanner's energy. On the one hand it was cute, but on the other hand, she didn't want him to make an enemy. This guy's energy showed that there was something to him that might just fit in perfectly with them. She was still hesitant, though, since she knew his dark swirling streaks could bring something very bad to a place where she only wanted to see light. Only time would tell.

"So, have you gotten any word on what the musical will be this year?" Emma asked Izzie as they hung up their dresses and got ready for bed.

Izzie nodded excitedly. "I'm not supposed to know this, but I overheard the professors when I was walking around before school started. Apparently, and don't quote me on this, we're doing *Beauty and the Beast*!"

Emma covered her mouth and tried to muffle the squeal. "Oh, my gosh! That is like my *favorite* movie. And last summer my mom took me to see the Broadway play before it ended again. I still can't believe they've been doing that play for so long. I think they said it was something like the fortieth anniversary of it being on stage."

Izzie smiled and shut her wardrobe. "It's amazing. I'm nervous about auditioning for it. I'm pretty sure that like the entire school is gonna try out. On top of that, there will be so many people in the audience that we're going to have to have multiple shows. It's a little overwhelming."

Emma shook her head. "You have to try out. You killed it as Dorothy last year. You can't quit now."

Across the room, Kathleen was talking to Alison about third-year classes. "What I'm really excited about is the magic we get to do this year. The spells are going to be huge, and the potions class is going to be insane."

Alison nodded and smiled. "I know, right? But remember, with bigger magic comes harder exams, which means more time studying and less time doing the things we like to do."

Kathleen sighed. "You have to be the bummer, don't you?"

Alison laughed and glanced at Aya and Jennifer's energy on the other side of the room. Aya was trying to make Jennifer feel welcome. She sat on the edge of Jennifer's bed and talked to her as she put away her things.

"I have this feeling that Ethan is sweet on you." Aya giggled.

Jennifer shifted and looked at her, lifting an eyebrow. "I kind of got that feeling too when he kept making me magical roses and horses that turned into smoke. It was cute, I can't lie. But I don't really know him."

Aya shrugged. "Ethan's a good guy. He gets into a lot of mischief, but he wouldn't be a part of our family if he didn't have a good heart. I've seen him stand up for people you'd never expect him to stand up for and change his views because he gave people a chance. Who knows? If nothing else, he's a really good friend to have."

When everyone fell asleep, Alison and Izzie wasted no time pulling on their shoes and sneaking out. They enjoyed the cool breeze that had lowered the temperatures after the sultry August afternoon. Alison used her senses to find the faeries whispering and dancing in the trees. Izzie looked up at the full moon and wondered where Luke was at that moment.

"Point out some of the things you're talking about from before the school was here," Alison requested excitedly. "I love that kind of stuff."

Izzie squeezed her hand, and the two set off over the field toward the barn. She stopped Alison about three hundred yards from the barn and turned her to the left. She pulled energy up and blanketed the remnants of an old building with her magic. Alison watched the energy wrap around the beams of the old chimney and smiled.

"That used to be the stable boy's residence. Apparently, it was a little one-room cottage situated so he was close to the barns and could take care of the horses. And across from that," Izzie said as she spun the magic to the left and covered the ruins of a larger building, "was apparently the servant's quarters. From what I read in the library, there were over thirty servants at one point. Over the years, when slavery was abolished and having servants went out of fashion, it dwindled to about two or three. When the house finally closed about fifty years later, those servants moved on to somewhere else. After that, the Fixer acquired it and held onto it, until finally, they turned it into the school."

"Wow, that's really cool!"

"Yeah. There are things like that all over the grounds,

but they're way cooler during the day, at least for me. I can use my magic to show them to you."

"I want to show you something," Alison said as she reached into her pocket and pulled out the amulet. "Shay gave this to me. She got it from a powerful gnome in LA."

"What does it do?"

"Apparently a lot of things, but right now it just focuses my energy. It makes everything much clearer, but it only works for short periods of time. I have to take it off after a while, or I get this crazy migraine. That's what it needs to recharge."

"That's really awesome. Does it help you control your magic?"

"It does, but mostly because it helps me see things clearer and lets me feel my magic before it explodes without me even knowing." Alison shrugged and put it back in her pocket. "I'm curious to see if I'll have to use it this year."

"Hopefully not, but it's definitely good to have. I could probably use something like that myself."

The girls continued to walk along, talking about the things that they wouldn't discuss in front of everyone else. In the background were the crickets, the bullfrogs, the tree frogs, and the cicadas, with the interesting addition of the sound of the dragon catching prey. The girls sat down in the grass at the edge of the woods and Izzie looked at the sky as she listened to the shifters howling somewhere in the distance.

"So, at the end of last year I had more memories, but I kinda kept them to myself. They've mostly been about this battle. It's the same memory I've had since the beginning.

I'm standing with that man and that woman, the ones who I have other short memories about, but in this one, they're fighting to protect me. On top of that, there are other memories. Things like having my hand held as a child or learning to use my powers. I didn't even think I knew about my powers or how to use them until I got to the school."

"That *is* strange." Alison sighed. "Maybe they are things from your past that for some reason your mind blocked out. Maybe there's a reason you don't remember them, like something bad happened. Sometimes I don't remember things from my past because of what happened to my mother, but like I said before, in time they come through."

"Maybe." Izzie sighed. "I'm convinced that something is just not right with my memory. For whatever reason, the things I'm supposed to know are real don't seem real at all. And the things that seem like dreams feel like real memories to me. I don't understand it."

"Okay," Alison replied, sitting up. "Tell me what you remember from the orphanage."

"I remember sleeping three to a room. It was a big house, I think. There were adults there, but I don't remember any of their names or faces. There were a lot of kids there too, but I don't remember their faces either."

Izzie quickly recalled all the memories that had been placed in her head. Alison immediately recognized that everything was general, not detailed. With her dreams, she could recall everything from what was happening to the color of the woman's shirt to the way the magic felt when it blew past her face. It was like things were backward.

"I wish I could help you with this," Alison said. "I can

see now why you're so confused. You can tell me every-thing about your dreams, but when it comes to your past, it's bits and pieces with no detail. When you talk about the orphanage I see it in black and white, but when you talk about your dreams, they're vivid, like I can almost see the energy of the people in them."

"I know," Izzie said dryly. "Like I said, it doesn't make any sense. I can only…"

Izzie sat straight up and looked around as the sound of barking and whining like a dog fight or a battle radiated from beyond the gates of the mansion. The girls sat there for several moments wondering what in the world was happening, then Izzie stood up quickly, and Alison followed, watching the fear and anxiety flow through her energy. Suddenly, she saw a flare of energy as Izzie pulled magic, held out her hands, and twisted a fireball.

"I can help them. I can use my magic and help the shifters. Whatever's after them has magic but they don't, and that's not fair…"

Alison grabbed her wrist, grounding Izzie's energy. "Izzie, Luke is going to be fine. He may not even be out there with them. Fighting with a dark family is not what you need to be doing right now. It's dangerous. I know you care about Luke. I feel the same way about Tanner, but Luke is stronger than you think he is. Trust me on this."

Izzie sighed and blinked the magic out of her eyes, letting her arms fall with Alison still clutching her wrist. She was impressed by how quickly Alison could ground her and pull her back to reality. Lately, when she got into a frenzy and started to pull up her magic, it almost felt like she was floating away with it. The light inside her had become so strong and powerful that it almost called to her, and whenever she was using it, she felt this peace that she couldn't explain to anyone else. There was no darkness inside Izzie. It was pure light, and that made controlling her powers more difficult.

"Come on, let's go see if Horace is up. If not, we'll head back early. I think you need to get some sleep tonight, Izzie. Maybe it will be good for you. Sometimes having a good rest helps you control your magic better."

Izzie stared at the gate, still hearing the wolves howling and barking in the background, but finally, she sighed and nodded. She desperately hoped Alison was right.

6

The freshmen boys hurried around their dorm rooms trying to get ready for class. None of them wanted to spend their first day in detention by not getting there before the second bell. Some of them were smart. They'd gotten up early and lounged around while the others ran around like chickens with their heads cut off. It was the same thing every year with the freshmen. They started the year in a frenzy, and by the end of it, most of them didn't care if they made it to class on time.

Connor, the same dorm proctor who had been there when Ethan and Peter were freshmen, came whistling down the old broad oak stairwell as he stopped on each floor to check on the boys. He was excited and optimistic about the new year as different students passed him on the stairs, heading toward breakfast. He always stopped by the freshmen level last, knowing they would take the longest to get under control, answer questions for, and fix whatever magical issues they were having. He loved and hated the beginning of each year. He enjoyed the new batch of students, but at the same time, he always wished they were a little bit more prepared.

"Morning, Connor," one of the upperclassmen said as he passed him, giving him a high five.

"Kamran, my man! You ready for the junior level potions making class this year?"

The kid looked over his shoulder as he went down the stairs and shrugged. "Ready or not, here I come."

"That's right. Be positive!"

When Connor made it to the freshmen floor, he turned to walk down the hallway but stopped when he heard liquid gushing. He tilted his head to the side and wondered if he could really be hearing a giant fountain. His eyes grew wider as the sound of water splashing onto tile echoed through the corridor. Several freshmen ran past, leaving wet footprints on the carpet. Connor pressed his hand to his forehead.

"Oh no, oh no, oh no."

He couldn't believe he was already dealing with pranksters. It was only the first day. He'd been at the school for quite a while and had seen his fair share of idiots, especially the upperclassmen, but to have freshmen pulling pranks on the first day? It was not a good start to the year. He let out a deep breath, knowing he had to keep his cool until he found the idiots. It was way too easy to send them to detention. He would definitely be coming up with something better, depending on the severity of whatever was going on down the hall.

When the freshmen shouts increased and the foot traffic heading for the stairs grew, he took off at a sprint and threw open the door to the floor. The noise got louder the closer toward the bathroom he went, and he cringed. At the end of the hall, some laughing freshmen boys stood wringing their hands and waving their wands ineffectually. As soon as Connor turned the corner, they scattered in different directions, but mostly down the hall toward the cafeteria.

"Don't go too far!" Connor yelled at them.

He walked slowly into the bathroom and peered at the mess, realizing that someone had jammed a frozen Boston cream pie in the toilet before flushing it. "Seriously? An entire Boston cream pie? Where the hell did they even get it?"

The first thing Connor did was trace the magic, finding exactly what stream of energy belonged to the prank. It actually turned out to be three very familiar strings of energy he had met just last night during the mixer. Something that the new students didn't always understand was that when it came to adults with magic, they could usually figure out who the culprit was, especially when it was a young and stupid teenage boy. He rolled up his sleeves and pulled out his wand.

"They're lucky I'm not going to make them eat this pie," he grumbled as he waved his wand and lifted the pie out.

He dropped it on the floor and let it splatter against the walls, then sent a strong burst of energy to push down the water that was spurting out of the toilet. He pressed the silver handle to flush it, which ended the chaos and flooding of the bathroom. Connor let out a deep breath and brushed his hands on his pants, looking down at the wet soles of his shoes.

"All right, everybody ran? I guess I have to figure this out on my own."

Downstairs, he found the freshmen lined up outside of the cafeteria. They'd tried to hotfoot to breakfast, but the upperclassmen had forced them out so they could go in first. Therefore, Connor didn't have to go searching through the cafeteria for them.

"You *do* realize that Boston cream pies don't belong in the toilet," he pointed out, walking up and down the line of freshmen boys. "All right, it's time to tell me who's responsible for the mess upstairs?"

They all looked at each other, and finally, everyone raised their hand. Every single one of them took responsibility. Connor admired that, especially on the first day of school when most of them were just trying to survive. He nodded and rubbed his hands together, then pointed at the stairs.

"All right. If you all want to take responsibility, then you all get to clean it up… Before you eat." The boys groaned but turned toward the steps. "Don't worry, boys, I'll save you some warm oatmeal. Oh, and welcome to the School of Necessary Magic!"

Alison and Izzie, with the gang right behind them, led the charge toward their first class of the day. It was Dark Magic 3.0 with Professor Xander Powell, and everyone was a bit nervous about what they'd face. Professor Powell was a great teacher, but it was no secret that he was a bit rough around the edges. On top of that, dark magic had been a touchy subject recently, with all the shifter issues and the dark families starting to come to the school. Suffice it to say, it wasn't everyone's favorite class.

"Do you think he'll talk about what happened last year?" Izzie asked.

Alison shrugged. "I don't know, but I *do* know that no matter how much we don't like this class, it's probably one of the most important we'll have this year. I've seen a lot darker magic floating around people's energy recently, especially this summer, and as recently as the train ride to the school. I think everybody needs to know how to defend themselves."

Izzie looked at Alison and raised her eyebrow, unsure what she was talking about in regards to the train ride. She knew Alison could see energy and souls, which meant she saw darkness before anyone else. It made her kind of nervous that Alison was seeing so much of it. Until recently, those who studied dark magic had stayed in the shadows, as they had for the last twenty years. Something had awakened them now, though; something that was making everyone nervous. She had noticed that every time Luke picked up a drink, he sniffed it first. He wanted to make sure that he wasn't going to drink anymore poison. She hated that he had to live like that. That *any* of them had to live like that.

When they walked into the class, the professor didn't bother to look up. He sat at his desk, grumpily reading a piece of paper. The girls plopped down next to each other in the second row, with the boys behind them. Even Ethan, usually late to everything, made sure to be on time to Professor Powell's class. He didn't want to feel his wrath.

As soon as the bell rang, the professor put his hands on the desk and stood up. Everyone was already quiet and waiting.

"Brian Lenders! Come up to the front, boy. Don't make me wait!"

The kid jumped from his seat and ran up to the front, nervously holding his wand in his hand. He knew that he was about to be the example for something. Professor Powell, looking more tired than usual, nodded to let him know to be ready. The class clutched the edges of their desks, wondering what was going to happen next.

"*Extendia Appendage!*" Professor Powell yelled, casting a simple dark spell to cause the boy's arms to grow from regular length to reach the ground.

The boy, with his wand up in the air, yelled a counter spell. "*Blockage...uh...Extendus!*"

The boy's counterspell hit Professor Powell's and split the magic in half. One side flew through the classroom and hit the backwall, sizzling as it sparkled down onto the floor, and the other half hit the boy in the arm. His right arm lengthened until his fingertips dragged the floor. The boy's eyes grew wide as he tried to lift his arm, but it was so heavy he couldn't. Professor Powell flicked his wand, and a mist of white magic circled Brian's arm and returned it to its original length.

"Half-measures will get you maimed, or worse, killed. You must *commit* to a spell!"

He nodded for the boy to go back to his seat and called up a few more students, trying simple dark spells on them. They were all so nervous and so scared of the professor that he got the same results from every single one of them

—they stuttered through a counter spell, receiving half of the blow of the dark magic. The professor was right, though. Half of a very serious spell would leave them maimed or killed. They needed to work on being less nervous and more prepared because Professor Powell, was not the worst thing that they would face.

"Alison, come up to the front."

Alison faced Professor Powell, watching the emotion that flowed through his soul. As soon as he flicked his wand, she saw the energy. She quickly put up her hands and instinctively countered him, surprising him and setting him back on his heels. He straightened his shirt, nodding.

"Well done, Alison." Alison knew he was impressed, even if everyone else saw only the scowl that never left his face.

The other students were grumbling, jealous that Alison was a Drow and could so easily face off with the professor. Izzie was tired of hearing it. Alison was special, which should be looked at as a positive thing. They shouldn't make her the butt of jokes. She flicked out several pea-sized fireballs and hid her smile as Alison's detractors jumped from their seats. She could tell it was going to be a really long year.

7

The next class was Multi-dimensional with Professor Rupert Wilson. It had ended up being most people's favorite class by the end of their sophomore year, and everyone was looking forward to the practical application portion this year. These would be real-world scenarios, things that could actually happen to them once they graduated and started their lives. They weren't necessarily simple things like not being able to open a jar, but were emergency situations in which magic was necessary despite non-magicals being present.

Professor Wilson had their glasses already set out on the desks when the students arrived but had not activated them just yet. He was curious to see how the students would do. He'd met some very interesting ones the year before. After listening to their reactions to real world historical situations and how they might change them, he was very interested to find out how they would respond when they were put into various circumstances in which magic was needed. It would also allow the students to understand their proficiency at magic and where they needed improvement.

"Welcome back, juniors. It's good to see so many bright, shining faces in the room. Some of you I don't recognize, but that's okay. We'll get to know each other soon enough."

He chuckled and rubbed his hands together, staring at the students. The new ones had no idea what they were in for.

"For those of you who may not remember, the topic is Multi-dimensional, focusing on real-world situations. Last year, we focused on historical perspectives but were unable to go very far since the class started so late in the semester. Today is going to be a fun day. Each set of glasses, once activated, will give you a real-world scenario that you may be faced with at some point. Your job is to get yourself out of that situation using magic, and you can replay the situation multiple times."

Professor Wilson walked up and down the aisles, tapping his wand on each desk as he activated the glasses.

"When you're in these scenarios, you will want to remember that no matter how chaotic it may seem, take a deep breath and simply ask yourself, what magic should I use? What about the bystanders who may be in or near the situation? If you get the answer wrong, that's okay. Restart and try something different. There are no right or wrong answers at this point. This is simply an exercise to allow you to understand what you need to work on, and where to go from here. This will not be the only time you do this exercise. You may begin."

The students excitedly put on the glasses, and immediately found themselves in different situations. Ethan, Peter, and Izzie all had the same one. They were jetting down a winding mountain road in a car, and the brakes weren't working. All three of them stabilized themselves and leaned back in their chairs.

Ethan grabbed the steering wheel and held on tight. He turned and jerked with each curve. Not only could he see what was going on, but he was also completely immersed in the situation. That included the terror that leapt into his chest as the car slid around a turn, almost tipping over the side.

"Take a deep breath, Ethan," he said to himself. "What spell would you use?"

The first spell he tried locked the brakes, which unfortunately wasn't a very smart idea. He ended up rolling the car off the side of the mountain.

"Holy crap," he shouted, ducking and grimacing until the screen went dark and the scenario started over. "Whew, I don't want to do that again."

Next, he attempted to fix the brakes while simultaneously using magic to move the vehicle. He thought it was working at first, and got super-excited when he heard the squealing of the brakes and saw the sparks of magic under the hood.

"Oh, yeah, mechanic on the go… Wait! Oh crap."

He looked up to find a semi barreling toward him from the opposite direction, and his car still wasn't slowing down fast enough. He panicked and jerked the wheel, which sent both him and the semi to the gorge below in a fiery blaze.

———

Peter was having a similar problem, although he used his mechanical knowledge to try to fix the situation. He attempted to fix the brakes as he was moving like Ethan had, but since he wasn't able to focus while keeping the car on the road, he ended up barreling into the side of the mountain and exploded with his car.

He ripped the glasses off and dropped them on the table with sweat pouring down his head. "Nope, this is ridiculous. Absolutely ridiculous. I just turned to ash."

"Relax, buddy." Ethan chuckled. "I've been ash like four times already. Eventually, it's like a video game."

Izzie breathed heavily, unable to control her emotions. She was plummeting down the side of a winding mountain road with no brakes, after all. She didn't know one person besides Ethan who *wouldn't* be nervous.

She'd gotten herself so riled up that she could feel the energy blowing through her. During her first attempt to fix the car she'd had zero control over her energy. Her magic burst from her, surrounded the car with light, and sent it careening over the edge. She clenched her eyes shut as the rocks came closer and closer to her windshield, and only opened them after the screen went black.

After several more tries with just about the same results, she took off the glasses. She was frustrated and looked around the room. She couldn't understand why she couldn't keep her emotions under control. She had faced dark wizards, but she couldn't face an out-of-control car?

Two rows over, Emma pulled her glasses off with a huff.

"Do you have the plane one?" she asked Jennifer with frustration.

"Yeah. I just blew up two hundred and fifty-three people by trying to land the plane on a giant bouncy house." Jennifer chuckled.

"Nice. I just killed everybody because I tried to land in a vat of Jell-O."

"What flavor?"

Emma laughed. "Blue raspberry. It's my favorite, so I figured, why not land it and have a snack too? I was wrong, though. I just ended up with a whole bunch of hot, dissolved Jell-O that stuck to the crash survivors and burned them to death. I would just like to note that jet fuel and Jell-O don't mix well."

Jennifer grimaced. "I'll keep that in mind. Wow."

They put their glasses back on and tried again. Emma decided that using magic to keep the plane level might allow the pilots to have a better chance of landing. To that end, she created a forcefield that leveled the plane out and allowed it to descend, even though she couldn't figure out how to slow it down. Her plan would've worked if she could have, but instead, the plane touched down and then flipped end over end because it was going much too fast.

"No, no, no!" Kathleen screamed from her chair.

She looked behind her, running at full speed as the

dragon chased her. His huge legs tensed and released as his claws dug into the ground, creating large craters beneath his feet. She huffed and puffed as she ran toward a large boulder and leapt over the top and ducked behind it. She pulled out her wand and looked at the long stick with wide eyes, then took a deep breath and jumped up, swishing her wand to create a force field between her and the dragon's fire.

"Yes!" she yelled as the fire bounced off her shield and evaporated.

The dragon shut its large snarling snout, snuffing out the fire, and Kathleen released the shield, smiling and smacking her hand on the boulder.

"And *that's* how it's done!" Kathleen was proud, but then tilted her head and listened closely.

There was a soft whimper , and she looked behind her at a town that had been set ablaze by the ricocheting flames. She just stood there for a moment, knowing she had two choices: put the fire out in the village, or protect herself.

"Ugh, of *course,* I get the one where I am supposed to be selfless."

She rolled her eyes and flicked her wand, sending a spray of water over the town. With that done, she closed her eyes and felt the heat wrap around her, ending her session and blacking out the glasses. She took them off for a moment and glanced at Aya, who was looking at her with a raised eyebrow. Apparently, she had the dragon one as well, and they were both thinking the same thing, Dorvu.

"Mhmm." Kathleen nodded and turned back around.

Aya put her glasses back on and found herself once more in front of the large dragon. Instead of running this time, though, she swirled the magic around her body and through the air to connect her and the dragon into a single large energy field. The dragon fought back at first, but she sent out calming magic and brought the dragon to his knees. Slowly, she walked forward, and the energy still swirled around them as she laid her hand on the dragon's head. He whimpered slightly but didn't move, entranced by the magic.

"Calm, little one," Aya whispered. "I'm not here to hurt you. I'm here to help you."

Aya's plan might have worked, except that she released the energy too soon. Immediately the dragon's eyes lost their glaze, and it swallowed Aya whole. That was definitely not the magic she had wanted to use. Aya pulled off the glasses and sighed, then looked over her shoulder at Alison, wondering which one she had gotten.

With the glasses firmly on her face, Alison looked around, surprised to find that the energy produced by the glasses was so strong that it created the images she needed to see. They weren't clear pictures like they were for the rest, but the energy shifted and created swirling arrays of colors that formed into their needed shapes.

She realized was standing on a tall building, and for a moment, she wasn't sure what her task was going to be.

Suddenly, everything started to shake beneath and around her, and the building began to crumble and shift apart. She jumped back, landing on her stomach, and started to slide toward an enormous hole in the roof.

"Shit!"

She took a deep breath and closed her eyes, realizing that she could do her magic just as well without the energy surges as she could with it. She allowed the energy to flow through her body and out of her hands and it surged over the top of the building and down the sides, swirling, winding, and pulling together the broken pieces to stabilize everything beneath her. It even wound through the hole, creating a magical barrier, so she didn't fall into the building.

She swirled a hand over her head and the magic pulsed and lifted her, which allowed her to hover over the side and slowly make her way down the building. As she lowered herself, she realized that there were people inside.

"Well, hell, I can't just leave them there." She sighed.

Alison pushed the energy from her chest, and her entire body shook as the strands of light swirled through the broken glass, wrapping around each person in the building. She pulled them out, and slowly lowered them to the ground to safety. There was nothing she could do to stop the earthquake, but she did get herself and everyone else out of the building and back far enough so that no one was hurt when it fell.

When the building had collapsed and no one had been injured, the session ended in her glasses, and she pulled them off. Once again, Alison had shone, but she didn't want anyone to know. She closed her glasses and held them tightly in her hand, trying to hide them from people. No matter how hard she tried, though, some people noticed that her glasses were no longer activated which meant she'd beaten whatever scenario had been programmed into them.

"Did you do it?" Izzie whispered.

"Yeah. Maybe I just had an easy one."

"Or you're Billy Bad-ass!" Izzie laughed loudly.

Alison might not have been proud of herself, but Izzie was extremely proud of her friend. Those real-world situations were nothing to scoff at, and she had been able to beat it the first time around. That didn't mean that she was better than anyone else, or that she was looking for praise. What it meant was that, in a real-world situation, she could save everyone's ass. Izzie fondled her glasses in her hands, not ready to try again. She knew that Alison and she were some of the strongest magical beings in the school, but they were unable to control their own magic.

Izzie shook her head, realizing that it wasn't that Alison couldn't control her power. It was that she couldn't control hers, and that made her wonder about them.

8

"Oh, look, Ethan! You just crashed a virtual car for Professor Wilson, and now you can crash a real one for Professor Powell." Kathleen laughed.

"I don't even know if I want to get behind the wheel of that thing," Ethan moaned. "I'm still recovering from bursting into a fiery ball."

"The feeling is mutual," Professor Powell grumbled, walking past them into the empty back parking lot.

It was driving class, and the professor was not pleased to have to teach it. He had gotten roped into being the instructor when Headmistress Berens had cashed in an old favor he owed her. He had tried to get out of it, but she just wasn't having it.

"A promise is a promise," the headmistress had told him.

He couldn't argue with that, but as he walked toward the gaggle of students, who were whispering and giggling to themselves in excitement, he was starting to question how important the promise had been. He cleared his throat and stood in front of them, lifting his hand to quiet the crowd. It took a moment for them to settle down. He was trying to have patience, considering this would be the first time for many of them to actually drive a car.

"I need everyone's full attention. You've managed to make it this far in driving class by passing the written exam given early this year, but I promise that if you can't make it through the driving part, I will not sign off for you to take your driving test when you turn sixteen."

All the students stood up straight now, listening to his every word.

"Driving is a great responsibility. Today, you'll get the chance to show me where your skill levels are, how responsible you are, and what you need to work on to pass the driving exam. Though I won't be in the car with you, don't forget that I have the ability to stop the car at any moment. Don't go showboating around. Now, pair up, and I'll call your name when it's your turn."

Everyone grabbed the person closest to them and whispered quietly while they waited for their turn. Izzie's group stood at the back. They were all slightly nervous about driving, except for Kathleen, who had been taking lessons from her father for years at that point.

"If I can drive my father's Mercedes, which is the love of his life, I'm pretty sure I can drive the school's 2010 Ford Focus around a parking lot full of cones." Kathleen giggled to Emma.

A loud crack drew their attention back to the course, which was set up near the fence behind the mansion. Tanner had managed to plow down three cones in one turn. He'd been going just a bit too fast, trying to show off for Alison's friends.

Jason smiled at first, quickly dropping it when Ethan looked back at him.

Professor Powell rolled his eyes, swished his hand to put the cones back up, and waited for them to switch positions. The other student climbed into the driver's seat, obviously more nervous than his friend. He carefully placed his hands on the three and nine positions and checked all his mirrors.

"I really hope I don't mow down any cones or take down the fence," Peter murmured nervously.

"Just don't go fast," Aya replied. "I don't think there's a speed requirement, and the slower you go, the more control you are going to have."

Peter shrugged. "I guess. My dad tried to teach me how to drive this summer, but he made me so nervous grabbing the 'Oh shit' handle and screaming every time a bird flew by that I didn't really get much out of it. Well, for except a nervous twitch every time I get near a car."

"You'll be okay, I promise," Aya assured him, trying to hold back a giggle as she slapped him on the shoulder.

The professor stood at the front nodding as a student maneuvered around the cones and pulled back up to the front, easing down on the brake and stopping in front of him. The kid put the car in Park and stepped out with a big smile on his face, but his friend grimaced, knowing he had failed miserably. The professor nodded and made notes on his clipboard before turning toward the group.

"Okay, Ethan. Try not to take the car down any winding roads and burst into fire."

Ethan took a deep breath and glanced at Luke as they walked toward the car. Luke sat down in the passenger seat, buckled his seatbelt, and looked at Ethan as he stared at the different knobs and wheels in front of him.

"I have to agree with the professor. Please don't turn us into a fiery ball."

"I think we're good on the fire part since I'm driving on a flat surface in a parking lot. Relax, I got this," Ethan said with a bit more confidence in his voice than before.

"That's what I'm afraid of," Luke replied, sighing is he clutched the seat.

Ethan put the car in drive and slowly pushed down on the gas, giving it enough juice to creep forward into the obstacle course. As he eased around the corners and steered carefully through the cones, it became very apparent that Ethan was a natural at driving.

"Huh," Luke chuffed as they drove toward the finish. "Who knew? I guess maybe you're just not a natural at figuring out how to stop your car from plummeting down the side of the mountain, but then, who is?"

Ethan pulled to a stop in front of the professor, smiling. He looked at Luke and nodded, proud of what he had just done. It wasn't often that he was the best at something, but so far, he seemed to be one of the best drivers in the class. The two boys got out, and the professor nodded, impressed, at Ethan as they switched places.

"Okay, wolfie." Ethan smiled. "Show me what you got."

Luke put on his seatbelt, took a deep breath, and put the car in drive. He lifted his foot off the brake, then pressed it hard again, lurching just inches forward. Ethan jerked forward and back in his seat and lifted an eyebrow as he slowly reached up and grabbed the handle above the door. Luke looked at him and smiled nervously, gripping the steering wheel harder.

"Take your foot off the brake, and just *slowly* press down on the gas," Ethan instructed.

Luke nodded. "I can do this."

He took his foot off the brake and shifted to the gas as he turned the car toward the lane of cones. As he stepped on the pedal, he pushed a bit too hard, and the car knocked down three of the cones. Ethan's hand flew up above the door, and he grimaced.

"Brake! Brake! Hit the brake!"

Luke gasped and took his foot off the gas, pressing hard on the brake. The moisture left on the pavement from the rain the day before caused the car to skid just slightly before he came to a full stop. Both boys jerked in their seats after the sudden halt. Ethan slowly looked at Luke, trying to hold back his laughter since the professor wouldn't be happy with that at all.

"Well, now that we're facing the finish line, why don't you just ease up on the brakes and slowly drift to a stop," Ethan said, glancing at the professor, who shook his head and flicked his wand. "I think that was enough practice for you for one day."

"I think you're right."

"Peace of cake," said Jason, smirking. "My uncle let me drive his car this summer."

Luke slowly drifted up to the finish line and once again braked too hard, bringing them to a sudden stop. He put the car in park, and the boys climbed out. Ethan chuckled and shook his head. Luke looked completely mortified.

"You magical people have it easy. If something goes wrong, you just flick your wrist and fix it. When it comes to driving, I'm no different than a human."

"Actually," the professor interjected, turning to the group. "Luke brings up a good point. When it comes to driving, none of us are any different than the humans. Using your magic while driving isn't going to do you any favors. There is no magical exam for the driving test. If you want to drive, you have to pass the human test, and that means without magic."

The professor paced back and forth in front of them, thinking about the best way to help them understand that using magic would actually impair them in the real world, at least when it came to driving.

"When you parallel park, you have to parallel park like anyone else. When you do a three-point turn, you have to do a three-point turn like anyone else. And, when it comes to knowing what the signs mean, no magic is going to help you there. The humans know we're out here, no matter how low a profile we try to keep, and they've taken steps to ensure that we are held to the same safety and technical measures that humans are. If you are found using magic during your test, not only will you fail and have to retake it, but when you *do* finally pass it, they will mark your license with an M in a circle to signify that you are a magical being."

The students whispered to each other, not having realized this. Almost all of their parents drove but none had an M on their license, which meant they had passed the test like a human. There were a lot of things that the students hadn't thought about when it came to living in the human world.

"It's best not to let on that you're magical when taking your test. It's not something you want on your license if you happen to get pulled over or are using it as identification in places where you don't want them to know." The professor looked down at his clipboard and made a note next to Luke's name. "All right, up next is…Peter."

Peter stepped forward, with Aya close behind him. The two of them got into the vehicle, with Peter behind the wheel. He was nervous. Aya kept quiet, knowing he needed that time to build up his courage to see the drive through. He eased off the brake and gently pushed on the gas, moving slowly forward. He was a cautious driver, which wasn't surprising to anyone watching. The only thing he usually wasn't cautious on were the spells that he did when he was working with organic substances.

They rounded the corners slowly and methodically, moving between each of the cones, and Aya looked at him and smiled. "I knew you could do it. Good job."

"Thanks," Peter said with a big smile as he came to a slow stop in front of the professor.

The rest of everyone went through their turn. Kathleen, of course, did fantastically. Aya was just as cautious as Peter, and Emma, while not quite as bad as Luke, definitely needed some practice. When it was Izzie's turn, she grabbed Alison's hand. Alison had been quietly standing to the side, watching the energy of the others grow more excited, telling herself it was okay she couldn't participate. She had tried to beg off and go to the library, her favorite spot where the gnomes would let her peek into a few of the older books not on the forbidden list.

But Izzie and Kathleen weren't having it and insisted she come along.

"Come with me. It'll be fun," said Izzie, encouragingly.

Alison gave in and let herself be pulled into the car, buckling her seatbelt with a smile.

"You ready for this?" Izzie asked excitedly. "I don't know why, but I feel like I've been behind the wheel of a car before."

At the last second, Jason opened the back door and scrambled into the seat, clapping on a seatbelt. "Let's go!" he said, smiling broadly, gripping Izzie and Alison's shoulders.

Tanner let out a protest, but no one moved to make Jason get out of the back, leaving Tanner fuming on the sidelines.

Izzie rolled her eyes as she shifted the car into drive and took off. She took the corners fast and without hesitation. The car whipped in and out of the cones as Alison cracked the window and laughed loudly, gripping the handle on the ceiling. Jason let out a whoop from the back, pounding the seat. Izzie took chances, and she wasn't slow, getting the job done without knocking down a single cone.

"Oh, my God," Alison exclaimed, laughing loudly when they came to a sudden stop at the finish line. "That was the best ride of my life. Can we do it again?"

The professor wiped his forehead and shook his head, reaching for the keys.

"I think that was more than enough for today."

9

"You ready for today?" Wyatt asked Henry as they walked with Luke toward Louper practice.

Henry scoffed. "You kidding me? I've practiced all summer and since school started, when everyone else was slacking. This match is going to be mine, and I hope we play with some of the newbies just for the fun of it."

"You guys should give them a break. Don't you remember what it's like to be new?"

"Don't go getting' soft on us, Luke. Getting picked on by the older kids is part of breaking into the Louper team." Wyatt laughed and clapped his hands together, obviously ready to give the younger kids hell.

"Yeah, well, I'm here to get better, and I want us to win the championship this year. I don't know if I'll have time to pick on younger kids."

"We want the championship just like anybody else," Henry ground out. "Maybe it's just because you're a shifter. I guess you'd know how it is to be picked on."

"No, he's just being a wimp and wants to suck up to the coach," Wyatt replied, rolling his eyes.

Luke, tired of the conversation, walked ahead of them as they approached the field.

He stood at the fence and watched as a few of the newbies who were trying out for the team were put through their paces on the field. Coach Regency had them running laps while throwing magical beams of light at them. He expected them to dodge and weave, as they would have to on a regular playing field. Unfortunately, there were only two of them who didn't land face-first in the mud while they were doing it. The coach was frustrated, and the rest of the team stood by laughing, the older kids having already been placed on the team.

"All right, newbies, take your place to the left side of the field. My assistant will get you started on what you'll be doing while the rest of the team gets ready for the upcoming game."

Coach Regency turned toward the older students and gestured to the right.

"The rest of you, line up over here. Our first game, which is in two weeks, will be against the Seattle Gargoyles. They are another private magical school, and they're nothing to be scoffed at. Unlike you slackers who took your summer vacations in the sand and sun, *that* team spent the summer playing out different game scenarios and readying themselves for the upcoming season. They are going to give you a run for your money if you don't buckle down and focus on what we're going to be doing here today."

Coach Regency looked down at his clipboard and

handed the test equipment for the newbies to use to the assistant. He tossed the clipboard to the side and cleared his throat, pulling out his wand. He had already decided he wasn't going to accept any shenanigans like the year before, not when they'd lost all hope of the championship in the first half of the season. Their school was known to be the best in almost everything, and Louper was not going to be the exception—not while he was the coach, anyway.

"Now, I decided not to use test spells. I'll be sending you straight into one of our normal championship scenarios. If you come out of this successfully, then we might actually have a chance at winning something this year. If you don't, we'll continue to practice, rain and shine, night and day, so that when you get out there you don't embarrass me. Our first scenario's going to be a dense forest, and you're gonna face all kinds of creatures, including dragons and wild animals. On top of that, there will be bogs, living trees, flying harpies, and pretty much everything else you could imagine in your worst nightmare. This is not a time for tourism, and don't slack off because you think it's just practice. No one's place on the starting team is assured, and I have no problem replacing you with one of the newbies."

Several of the players looked at each other, surprised to hear the coach say that. Then again, they assumed that if they couldn't beat the scenario, he wasn't going to give them the satisfaction of ending their school year as a starting member of the Louper team. That statement alone shook some sense into most of the players—except for Henry and Wyatt, who figured they were untouchable no matter what they did. Luckily, both played their hardest every time they were inside the scenarios, and even though Coach Regency didn't like their attitudes, he knew they would bring out the best in the team.

"Okay, boys, are you ready?"

Coach Regency swirled his wand over his head, not even waiting for a response. The bright beam of green light shot up into the sky, then flowed down over the students. They readied themselves by closing their eyes and waited for the magic to take hold. When they opened them again, they were exactly where they'd been told they would be: in a dark, dense forest with steam rising from the bogs and wild animals screeching in the background.

"Okay, there's no time to dillydally. We need to be on our A game. This is red versus blue, and you guys got me and Luke," Henry said, nodding at Luke. "This year, to try something different, instead of three groups, we're just gonna send out two. I'm gonna head up one group, and Luke's got the other."

All the guys looked down at their red jerseys as either an L or an H appeared on the front to signify who they were following.

"The guys with the L obviously are gonna follow me," Luke said, looking at Henry who was surprised that he took control but was not upset. "The rest of you will follow Henry. My group, we are going to head to the east and make our way through the forest, while Henry's group is gonna set off to the west. We'll circle around and meet back up at the edge of the forest, where I'm pretty sure we'll find either a clue or the treasure waiting for us."

Henry nodded. "Remember, we play as a team. If you see someone in trouble, you try to help them even if it means you get booted from the game. We win or lose together. There are no individual players in this."

The guys put their hands in the center and gave their battle cry before splitting into their groups. Luke motioned for his team to follow him to the right, staying low as they crept through the thick forest. Overhead they heard the screech of a harpy as she flew over the canopy to look for the players below. Luke reached an area where some trees were down, and he held up his fist to stop the team in their tracks.

"You see that group of trees right in the center? They are living, and I don't mean just like a normal tree. If you get close to them, they'll grab you and pull you down into their roots. Watch."

Luke snatched up a stick and threw it as hard as he could, and it bounced off one of the trees. Their eyes grew wide as the tree grabbed the stick with a growl. Luke crouched back down and looked at the others.

"We'll skirt around those trees to the right, but keep your eyes open. There are plenty of other animals out here ready to attack."

The team moved quietly around the trees, keeping low until they were finally past. However, in their need to get around that threat, they failed to notice the large group of cats perched just to the left of them in a tangled swatch of bushes. Just as the last team member walked past, Luke heard a scream and whipped around to find the cats demolishing half his guys.

"Get down! Use your magic!"

Some of the team members pulled out their wands while others used their elf magic to send out streaming bands of white light. The light tangled around and through the group of cats, pulling them to the ground and pinning them. They struggled to keep them under control as a wizard swished his wand, sending the beasts into unconsciousness.

The remaining team members stumbled back to Luke, breathing heavily and shaking their heads.

"They got half of us, if not more," one of the guys complained.

"That's the game. We keep going," Luke said pointedly.

The guys trekked around the circle, facing several different beasts but taking them down without losing any more players. When they reached Henry, however, they could see that he hadn't been as lucky.

"I only have two guys left," Henry told Luke. "We got attacked by a group of harpies only about ten minutes into the game."

Luke nodded. "I get it. We got attacked too. But the good thing is, I can hear the sparks that indicate the treasure right over there. Let's not waste any time, just grab it and get the hell out of here."

Henry motioned to the rest of the guys into the clearing. Without thought, several of the guys ran forward, only to find themselves sinking quickly in the bogs that surrounded it. Shortly thereafter their heads were completely submerged.

Luke swatted Henry in the chest, then lifted up a long, thick plank and threw it down across the bog. Henry nodded and slapped him on the shoulder, taking the first walk across. One by one, the boys crossed the bogs while looking down at the bubbling deathtrap beneath them.

When they had all made it, they patted each other on the shoulders, figuring they were about to take the treasure.

"One thing none one of you seems to have realized," Wyatt yelled from the center of the clearing, which got everyone's attention. "When you're trying to survive this game, you also have to remember that the other team is too. In this case, it looks like we were just the better team."

Henry growled and bolted across the clearing as Wyatt laughed and touched his hand to the treasure. By the time Henry got there, he was running across the empty playing field while Wyatt stood there beaming from ear to ear and holding the trophy. Wyatt had been the only one of this team to survive, but he had used his keen intellect and the navigational skills he'd acquired during the summer to get him to the treasure before Henry.

"Well, at least we were close." Luke chuckled, watching Wyatt's victory dance.

"Yeah, at least we aren't them," one of the other guys said about the newbies across the field.

"From the looks of it, they got the top version of the game." Luke laughed.

That was exactly what the newbies had gotten. Wearing their goggles, they stood in different parts of a corn maze through which they had to try to find their way to the treasure in the center. Unfortunately for them, they kept running into toddlers who would kick at them and scream, which would bring angry parents, hornets, and mice—the worst combinations they could think of. To everyone else, though, they just looked like a bunch of bumbling idiots.

10

"Shouldn't you guys be on your way to class?" Scarlett asked with an air of superiority as she walked up to a group of freshmen, who were comparing notes and laughing.

"Yes, ma'am," one of the students said before rushing off quickly.

Scarlett shook her head, rolled her eyes, and looked back at those who were following her like groupies. "See? You have to keep order, or you're just gonna have chaos all the time, with these little freshmen running around doing whatever they want."

She spotted a group of sophomores whispering quietly to each other in the corner and tapped one of them on the shoulder.

"So, what we have going on here? It looks like someone has a secret."

The girl folded up a piece of paper and put it in her pocket defiantly.

"Nothing, Scarlett. We were just on our way to class."

Scarlett scrunched her nose. "Fine, if you don't want to let me in on your secret, then just expect that I won't be letting you off the hook anytime soon."

Scarlett was exercising her new role as Student Body President, but she seemed to think there wasn't anything more to it than bossing people around and nosing into other people's business. As she and her groupies walked toward her next class, she talked constantly, the group hanging on every single word that she spoke.

"Of course, what we will absolutely be doing is getting better snack machines in here. No one wants to spend their afternoon sitting next to someone who just ate sour cream and onion potato chips."

The group mumbled to each other and shook their head in agreement, even if they didn't agree.

"And these classes, they need to be shorter. Sometimes I find myself so bored that I consider just leaving. It's a waste of time, in my opinion. We could be in the kemana, seeing what real life and the magical world are instead of learning stupid spells that we'll never use."

She stopped and turned toward the group.

"And on that subject, we absolutely need to have more passes to the kemana. This limitation is absolutely ridiculous. They call it our free time, but it's really not free. It's whatever they want it to be."

Standing at the other end of the hallway, Headmistress Berens leaned against the doorway and tapped her foot, listening to everything Scarlett was saying. She raised an eyebrow when she realized that Scarlett had no idea what her responsibilities were as Student Body President.

"Scarlett! I want to see you in my office, please," the headmistress yelled at her.

Scarlett jumped slightly, understanding that Headmistress Berens had been listening all along. She smiled and nodded at the others, then hurried toward her as the headmistress turned toward her office. Scarlett was quiet as she closed the door, and she stood with her hands in front of her as the headmistress took a seat behind her desk.

"Scarlett, on several occasions, I've listened to what you've said about the so-called important things that need to be changed at the school. I think that perhaps you do not completely understand what a Student Body President is…and is not. You need to focus on the well-being of the students, not what snacks they eat or what they get to do in their free time. Your role is to ensure that the entire student body has a fluid and successful school year. On top of that…"

The headmistress stood and walked over to the window with her hands clasped in front of her as she looked out at the students in the courtyard.

"*Your* success is just as important. You need to be focusing on your grades, and your college applications, since you're a senior. You are a smart and talented young lady, and you have a natural ability to lead people. You should use that for the betterment of society, not for what you've been doing. I want to see you live up to your potential, and I promise you that you won't leave here with a bad reputation."

"Yes, headmistress," Scarlett said, lowering her head.

She knew what the headmistress was saying was true, but she didn't want to admit it.

"Good," the headmistress replied, turning to her with a smile. "I look forward to seeing what you can do with this year and this role."

———

At the end of the day, students ran all over the school. Some headed to study hall, others retired to their dorms, and a large group went off to the different clubs that were meeting. In one of the classrooms at the end of the hall, the Entrepreneurs Club was meeting. Each was excited to show what they'd worked on through the summer and talk about what the year would bring for their new creations.

"So," one of the girls started when it was her turn, "one of the most time-consuming things in the morning for girls is putting on their makeup. There have been times that it's taken over an hour to apply everything, especially with the number of people who go in and out of the bathrooms in the mornings. So, this summer, I created a machine that puts your makeup on perfectly every single time."

The girl switched on the machine which hummed quietly and had lights beaming all around it. She pulled her hair back into a ponytail and cleared her throat, then leaned toward the machine.

"All you have to do is select the setting for the type of makeup that you want to be applied. All of them are customized to the person who is purchasing the machine and their skin color, etc. You press this button, and you rest your chin and forehead on the very comfortable padding on the front. Then…"

The girl leaned her head against the machine and closed her eyes as several gadgets inside clinked and ticked. About three minutes later, a soft bell chimed and the girl pulled back, revealing perfectly-applied makeup. The only thing that was off was that her blush was just a little bit too bright.

"Voila! A perfectly applied face within three minutes. Think about all the things we could get done in that extra hour. Of course, it still needs a little bit of tinkering—don't want to walk out of the house looking like a porcelain doll with bright red cheeks—but all in all, it works very well. You can also use any type of makeup that you want."

Several of the girls oohed and ahhed, while the boys rolled their eyes. The guys didn't see any real need for something like that, but then again they wouldn't. One of the guys stepped up and waved his hand.

"Enough of this girly stuff. We've got some real inventions to show. From the beginning, we've wanted to build robots. I mean, who doesn't want to build robots?"

The girls crossed their arms, as the boys pulled out some of the robots they had in progress. Most of them didn't do much. They walked around, picked things up, and made crude jokes that the boys had downloaded into their systems.

"That is *so* 2010," one of the girls said. "In Japan, they have robots as personal assistants."

One of the other girls nodded. "Yeah, and they can teach your children instead of sending them to schools. I'm afraid you boys are slow on the go with this one."

"We're just getting started," the guy defended. "Give us some time, and we will blow that other technology right out of the water."

"Uh huh," the girl said, giggling and rolling her eyes. "Just so you know, a machine like this actually is a robot. It does everything a girl would want a robot to do."

Before the group could start arguing, Grace stood up and raised her hand. "Okay, okay. Everyone settle down. I want to show you what I came up with this summer. My father owns a 3D printer, but it can only make smaller things like signs and containers. To give it credit, if you set it up right you could build a car, but I wanted something bigger—something that built things that were effective and inexpensive for the public. I created this 3D printer that can build houses."

Everybody watched in shock as Grace pressed buttons on the 3D printer and produced the necessary pieces in the order they needed to be put together. There were small parts like screws, bolts, and nuts, and there were larger parts like doors, windows, and the walls of the actual building. She had scaled it down for presentation, knowing she couldn't build a full-size house inside the school, so instead she'd decided to build a three-foot-tall dollhouse.

"Now, this is obviously smaller than a real house. I made it that way on purpose. It wouldn't do me much good to build a real house inside the mansion, and I couldn't get the headmistress' permission to build one on the grounds until the machine was confirmed as perfectly safe. So, instead, I decided to build this dollhouse as a representation of what this 3D printer can do."

Everyone gathered around as she put the pieces

together, screwing down the floors and connecting the walls with the separate little pieces that had been printed out. When she was about halfway done, she stopped and looked at the rest of them.

"My goal is to enter into the National Scholastic Contest in the spring. I brought it here because I wanted you guys to help me work out the bugs. Once we show it's viable through the miniature house, the headmistress will allow us to build a full-sized model on the grounds. This material is non-toxic and can either be colored to produce whatever you want or painted once assembled. What you guys think?"

For a moment everyone hesitated, too enthralled by what they were seeing to actually say anything, but after a few moments, they erupted in excitement, which filled Grace with pure pride and the motivation to take the school to the win in the scholastic competition.

11

"Shhh! You don't want them to figure it out, do you?" one of the boys hissed.

"No, but I still think we should have taken the Bug instead of the Forrester. We are just asking to be caught," one of the other boys whispered.

"Stop worrying. Just keep pushing."

Several of the junior boys had broken into the garage on the outskirts of the school property and nabbed one of the school cars—an old Subaru Forrester. They figured that if they were able to get it out, they could practice for the next class and even mess around a little bit with their friends. They all knew it was completely against the rules, but they figured they only had one chance at it, so why not?

"We're gonna blow the professor away at our next driver's ed class," one of the boys said.

"Yeah, and before the day is done, I'm gonna to do some sort of mad doughnut in the parking lot."

"Lord, please don't. That is just the kind of thing that's

gonna get us caught in about two seconds. I imagine we won't even make it through the whole thing without getting caught, but we don't need to *try* to draw attention to ourselves."

"You need to chill and just have some fun, for God sake. It's just a car! How much trouble can we really get into? It's not like we're taking it off the property or anything."

As the boys reached the top of the hill, they stopped pushing and looked out over the empty parking lot. Two of the boys clapped their hands and jumped into the front seats, excited to get started. The one in the driver's seat smiled at the other and started the car, rubbing his hands on the steering wheel.

"Now all we need to do is pretend there are cones out there."

The other boy sighed and rolled his eyes, then pulled out his wand. "Seriously, you would think that you forget you're magical. I'll just spell some cones out there. We don't even have to worry about running into them, because they're magical."

"Good thinking."

He put the car in drive, slowly let off the brake, and pressed lightly on the gas. The car moved forward at a glacial pace. His passenger leaned against the window making a face as if he didn't have all day to wait. The kid driving chuckled and pressed harder on the gas, speeding through the parking lot until it was time to take the turn to weave in and out of the cones. Unfortunately, he didn't realize how fast he was going and when he hit the brake, the back end swung around, and the car jolted to a stop.

"Whoa there, racecar driver. Don't take down the

fence."

"Hey, *you're* the one who told me to chill out."

"Yeah, well, I'm still worrying. Don't take us off the end of the world just because you don't know how to drive."

"Just relax. I've done this a hundred times at my parents' house."

He weaved in and out of the cones, nailing every single one of them and sending up sparks from the magic. He turned the last corner and stopped, looking at the guy in the passenger seat. The guy rolled his eyes and rubbed his hands down his face.

"You may want to ask your parents to actually teach you how to drive. I'm pretty sure you left marks on the pavement back there, which is a surefire way to get us caught. Get out and let me drive."

All the boys took turns. Some played around and almost caused them to get caught, while others carefully maneuvered in and out of the cones. Either way, it was most likely only a matter of time. The question was, would they fess up to being the ones who stole the car, or would they allow the entire class to pay the price?

Peter leaned against the wall, listening to the school newspaper's editor give all the newbies a rundown. It was his second year on the school newspaper, and he was hoping that he would get to report on something more exciting than just a chance encounter at the go-kart races. He felt like he had earned the right to be given an assignment with a little bit of danger and excitement.

"You're Peter, right?"

Peter looked at the senior, the shifter who was the editor-in-chief that year, and raised an eyebrow. He knew full well that they'd had conversations last year, but he still didn't remember who Peter was.

"Yeah, I'm Peter. You got a job for me?"

"I do," the senior said, excitedly flipping through his papers. "I just gotta find it. Hold on one second."

Peter hoped that whatever he picked out was a little more exciting than the one on top, which involved showcasing the Entrepreneur Club's newest inventions. Finally, the editor handed him the piece of paper.

"Here it is—your first job of the year. They put in new lines down in the parking lot, and I want you to report on it. You know, talk to the maintenance guy, explain why they were needed, and try to make it an exciting story."

Peter raised an eyebrow and looked from him to the paper and back again, feeling like he was messing with him.

"Seriously? You want me to report on lines painted on the parking lot?"

The editor sighed and shrugged. "It's the beginning of the year. Nothing too exciting is going on yet, and *someone* has to report on it."

Peter begrudgingly nodded, and the editor walked away. He grabbed his bookbag and shoved the paper inside, then pulled out his notebook, but he had no idea what he would end up writing. Hopefully, he could get some interesting shots, but he wasn't sure how interesting he could make pavement look.

"Hey, dude," Ethan called as Peter walked out of the

room. "Want to go grab something from the cafeteria?"

Peter sighed and shook his head. "Nah. I gotta get on this story so it can be turned in on time. I'll catch up with you later."

Ethan nodded and headed off as Peter made his way outside. The new lines were in the parking lot where they had been practicing driving, so he went to the back of the property and walked along the fence that paralleled the woods. He turned toward the parking lot, taking a couple pictures with this phone. Suddenly, from the woods behind him, he heard several voices. He put his phone back in his pocket as he scooted along the edge, making his way to investigate.

On the back corner were several English boxwoods that gave enough cover for Peter to hide there. He fully expected it to be several seniors or juniors plotting something that they weren't supposed to do, but to his surprise, the trio of voices all sounded older, and none of them up to any good.

The first voice was deep and raspy and had a sense of urgency. "Regardless of what we decide, we need to get into the school, and soon. It wasn't that long ago that we were sitting in the graveyard discussing this exact thing, yet nothing has been done."

The second voice was ominous and calm, speaking in a low tone. "Things *have* been done. We just have to figure out exactly how and when is the best time to break into the school. We can't just go running in completely unannounced. The professors here may be light magic, but they aren't fools, and they know how to use magic. I personally don't want to get caught up with them if I don't have to."

The first wizard scoffed. "Yeah. We already tried one thing and failed miserably. We're lucky they didn't trace it back to us."

"No one could have seen that coming. The toombie was a sure thing, or at least we thought it was. Whoever created the spell made it strong enough. The kid should have been dead before anyone had an opportunity to save him. We definitely misread someone in that school, because it would've taken a very powerful magical being to figure out the kind of spell that was wrapped around that boy. No one could've predicted that failure."

A gruff-toned wizard spoke. "Regardless, it failed, so now we have to move on. Where are we with these wards?"

One of the three stepped closer and looked around, not seeing Peter hiding in the bushes. "It's going well so far. We've gotten through the first ring of wards, with just one setback."

"Funny what you call a setback."

The second wizard pulled up the sleeve of his robe, showing a burn that went from his elbow to the tips of his fingers. It looked rough, but Peter could see the magic flowing around it, obviously taking the pain away and healing it faster than it normally would have. Whoever these wizards were, they were dark, and they were extremely powerful.

"We must be getting closer. If I didn't know better, I'd swear a wizard from one of the old families put up these spells. Someone has some pretty old books at their disposal."

Peter carefully took a step to the side making sure not to crunch any leaves or break any branches. He leaned forward, trying to get a better look through the chain-link fence at whoever was on the other side, but it was no use. He was unable to see their faces, given the way they'd positioned themselves in the trees and brush.

The gruff wizard cleared his throat and shuffled his feet in the leaves. "We'll talk about this later. Right now, we need to get out of here. For now, keep up your efforts—and try to keep your limbs intact and the small fires to a minimum."

Peter looked back in the direction of the school. *I should go sound the alarm, tell someone.*

He took a step back as one of the wizards with a long-hooked nose seemed to peer into the darkness straight at him.

He froze where he was, holding his breath.

"Of course, we have to be careful that no one finds out how much progress we're making," said the wizard.

"That's simple," said the gruff wizard. "We leave no tattlers behind."

"Good thing we have friends on the inside, even if they couldn't remove the damn spells. Someone gets wise to us, we'll hear soon enough."

"It's gotten us this far. They think they've got us beat. Only made 'em soft," cackled the wizard.

"How come we aren't in some bar? Whose idea was it to tramp through the woods?" grumbled a wizard.

"Hard to test the spells from a bar, you idiot."

"Just sayin'. Beer, warm seat."

"You're killing me."

Peter swallowed hard. *They have a mole! A traitor!* He

could feel his heart pounding as he listened, hoping to get some kind of clue. *Is it a teacher? A student?*

He couldn't imagine anyone he knew capable of betraying all of them. He wondered how he could tell anyone. Better he try to find out more, first.

Peter waited until the three men blended into the woods and stepped back out into the parking lot. He looked down at his empty piece of paper and back across the lot. He realized that in the wake of these wizards' appearance, he hadn't even thought about the article he needed to write. He sat down on the concrete ledge and put his elbows on his knees, leaning forward.

"There's so much more going on here, and I have to write this stupid story," he said to himself.

He slapped his hand against his forehead. "You're a journalist, dude," he whispered. "Okay, maybe just a high school journalist, but a journalist all the same."

One of the requirements was to write a story by taking one that might not be exciting and create something people would want to read. He started jotting ideas quickly in his notebook. Instead of a story about the lines, he was going to write a story about how many years the parking lot had been there, how many generations the students had used it, and what they had gone on to after leaving the high school.

Peter smiled and nodded. "Nice. I'll add a little emotional touch here—what exactly it's like when you first pull up in the parking lot, and what it must be like when you pull out for the last time."

He knew he had to put something in there about the new stripes, so he jotted down some notes about the painting that would be done by the gnomes who worked at the school. When he was done, he sat back, then looked over his shoulder at where he'd stood and listened to the wizards. He had come up with a great idea for the article, but in truth, it was the dark wizards he wanted to investigate. He had no idea how.

He looked down at the pavement between his feet, feeling almost exhausted. "I don't even know who to ask for help…"

"At least the weather's nice today," Alison remarked as she and Izzie strolled along on one of their nighttime walks.

"Yeah," Izzie agreed. "It's really quiet too."

The girls enjoyed their stroll through the fields toward the barn. However, before they could make the left, they looked toward the fence line. Alison put her hand out and stopped Izzie, pointing in the direction of the fence line. Izzie didn't see anything at first, but Alison saw the very vibrant and familiar colors of Peter's energy.

"It's Peter," Alison said taking off toward him. "I can see his energy."

Izzie grasped Alison's hand as they hurried. She was interested to find out why Peter was out so late near the fence.

"Hey," Alison said, touching Peter on the shoulder. "What are you doing out here?"

Peter sighed and looked at the two of them. "If my mind wasn't so busy right now, I'd ask you the same thing, but I'm pretty sure you guys come out here all the time."

Izzie nodded. "What's on your mind?"

"I don't know if I should say, not before I have more proof…"

Alison shook her head. "One thing I've learned is that when you have something that's weighing that heavily on your mind, you should probably let your family know."

Peter looked at her for a moment, then sighed, letting his arms fall to his sides. "You're right. So, I was out earlier in the parking lot beside the school. You know, where we practice for driving class? Anyway, while I was there, I heard voices and saw the figures of three dark wizards talking about entering the school, and how they were responsible for the toombie. I wanted to do some more research just to make sure that it was actually legit before going to the headmistress."

Izzie rubbed her chin. "I agree with you. This is serious stuff, but we need to find out more before we tell anybody else about it. What are you doing out here?"

"I thought maybe if I walked the fence line I'd hear them again or find them, but all I've heard is Dorvu up in the trees, and every once in a while, Horace calling his dog. I don't think they're around anymore."

"I have really good hearing," Alison said with a smile. "Why don't we walk with you? If there's something out there, I promise I'll hear it."

As they walked along the fence, they listened closely, but again heard nothing except Dorvu and Horace. Whoever was out there—whoever was trying to get to them at the school— had backed off, at least for the night. Peter knew he had to figure out who it was, though, and he had to do it before another attack occurred.

Alison and Tanner sat inside of Mya's on Main, a local Charlottesville restaurant that was much nicer than most of the places the students went to eat. They chose to have their date in town instead of in the kemana, figuring it would give them some alone time where no one from the school would bother them. The place was simple but elegant, with white table cloths, water goblets, and delicious food. It had everything that enhanced a really good date, including the company.

"I hope you don't mind being alone with me on a date." Tanner chuckled, taking Alison by the hand. "I just wanted somewhere that was gonna be quiet and chill and give us a chance to get to know each other better, now that we're together in person."

Alison smiled and shook her head. "I don't mind at all. It's actually nice to look around and not see any energy I recognize. Except yours, of course. And I agree. I think we really need to get to know each other better. With everything going on at the school in the last year or so, we've been so busy and so wrapped up with everything else that we couldn't take the time to just be together and understand each other."

Tanner smiled as the waitress arrived. "We'll start out with the mushroom plate and your pimento cheese."

"Very good, sir," the waitress responded, smiling at the two of them and walking away.

"Look at you," Alison teased. "Ordering for us and everything."

"I thought it might be easier." He chuckled. "I forget sometimes how self-sufficient you are. How nothing stands in your way."

"I don't mind." Alison chuckled, squeezing his hand. "It's nice having someone who wants to take care of me, even though I can more than adequately take care of myself."

"Well, I would never insult you by insinuating that I was going to take care of you, but I will always be here to try to make things easier," Tanner replied kindly.

"That's sweet." Alison smiled. "So, tell me about you. Tell me what it was like to grow up in the orphanage. Neither of us has parents, but I didn't go to an orphanage like you or Izzie."

Tanner took a deep breath and shrugged, squeezing her hand as he remembered she couldn't see that. "The orphanage was different than what you see in movies. I wasn't begging in the streets, and I wasn't beaten up by any of the other boys, but it was quiet and lonely. When I look back, I feel like my life was in black and white, and I was just breathing to survive with no real idea of what the future would hold. You would see boys come and go, being adopted then being brought back, and new ones coming in, and you would always wonder if you were next or if anybody would ever love you."

Alison looked at him with caring and squeezed his hand, leaning forward. Tanner laughed and shook his head.

"It wasn't as bad as my melodrama is making it sound. It was just kind of surreal. When I got out to the real world and saw that things were in color, that there were options no matter where I came from, all of it started to fade, almost like it was from another life."

Alison smiled, thinking of Izzie and the very few memories she had of the orphanage she'd come from. She immediately felt deep gratitude that she had been adopted by Brownstone and that she had Shay Carson there to support her.

"I guess if I was going to have to be in a situation like that, I kinda won the jackpot by being taken in by my dad and Shay. I sometimes forget that."

"Well, whatever the road that brought you here, I'm glad that we get to walk the future road together." Tanner smiled, lifting Alison's hand to his lips.

"Me too. You were definitely a surprise, but one that I would never give back."

The night air was beautiful, and the stars twinkled brightly in the sky. It was cold; chilly really, and not as late as it seemed. Alison and Tanner were more than happy to go for a walk in the quiet of Charlottesville hand-in-hand. They hadn't gotten much alone time, and they both desperately wanted it.

"I'm excited about the first Louper game," Alison said, squeezing Tanner's hand as they walked.

"I am too. Hopefully, it's not against those tyrants from last year."

"I know, right?"

Jason Parker and some of his dark wizard friends came laughing out of a local restaurant. Jason stopped and looked at Alison and Tanner with a grin. "Oh, look what we have here! Tanner the orphan boy. Looks like you're out for a lovely leisurely stroll."

"Back off, Jason," Tanner replied, rolling his eyes and pulling Alison to the left.

Jason and his friends laughed, and Tanner scooted closer to Alison. "Hi, Alison. You look beautiful tonight. Too bad your company doesn't match."

"Screw off, Jason," Alison replied, shaking her head at his dark energy. "Your jealousy is showing."

"Yeah, right." Jason laughed, looking slightly embarrassed.

"Leave her alone," Tanner replied, putting his arm between them.

Jason looked at him, then back at his friends. "Big man thinks he can bark orders. Oh, wait. I guess the barking is left to your little buddy, Luke."

Alison took a puff of air into her lungs and held it for a moment, balling up her fists. She was getting really tired of

Jason and people like him. They were about to ruin her evening. With every thought, she got angrier, until finally she dropped Tanner's hand and flung hers out in front of her.

"Alison…" Tanner called urgently, but it was too late.

"Woahhhh," Jason yelled as Alison lifted him into the air, then swiped her hands to the right, tossing him into a patch of grass.

He bounced off the ground and slid to a stop, looking up in shock at Alison. His friends scattered in different directions as Alison stepped toward Jason, watching the embarrassment and anger swirl around in him.

"Okay, okay." He put his hands up. "That is severely against the rules, but it looks like no one else saw."

"Leave me and my friends alone, Jason," Alison snarled.

Jason looked back and forth, but there was still no one around. Even his friends were gone. He picked himself up and brushed the dirt off the seat of his pants, then let out a deep sigh, turning back to Alison.

"Look, I… I wasn't trying to piss anyone off," he said quietly.

"Is that an apology?" Tanner scoffed.

Jason darted his eyes angrily toward Tanner and back to Alison, softening his look when he realized that she just wasn't having it.

"I'm sorry," he said grudgingly.

Tanner placed his hands on Alison's shoulders. "Come on."

"He just made me so mad." Alison wrung her hands together, staring down at where Jason had been sitting. He was long gone by that point.

Tanner nodded and slid his hand down her arm, grasping her wrist. "I know, but let's not let him ruin everything. Come on, let's go to the kemana."

Alison turned her head in the direction of Tanner's energy and smiled. "You're right, let's continue this date."

The two of them made their way to the bus station and sat close, watching out the window as the fields passed. When they arrived at the school, they made their way to the entrance to the kemana and down the stairs into the underground city. Neither of them wanted to face everyday life at that moment. They were enjoying their time too much to worry about it.

"It's definitely a different group of people in Ruby Falls at night," Tanner said, enjoying how tightly Alison held his hand.

"I can see the difference in energy, but there aren't as many dark people as I assumed there would be. There are just more people either in a hurry, or excited to be out."

"Why don't we get coffee and just people-watch? Or energy-watch, as you do it." Tanner smiled and kissed Alison on the forehead.

They walked into the uncrowded coffee shop and ordered two hot chocolates, including mounds of whip cream. Alison followed Tanner's energy to the outdoor seating and sat across from him. She watched the energy around her, from the faeries with their tiny glittery sparkles to the large Kilomea with their half-dark and half-light energy.

Tanner loved it down here. Ruby Falls had so many different shops filled with such interesting things, and then there were all the different magical beings. He couldn't remember a time in his life when he had been that comfortable in a place.

"It's nice to be around our people. Don't get me wrong, I love humans. I mean, I grew up with them, but I'm more comfortable around magicals," Tanner whispered.

"You know, after living most of my life in the human world—remember, I didn't know my mother was a Drow princess until recently—I'd have to agree with you. If for some reason I had to use my magic down here, no one would bat an eye, and I wouldn't start an international incident."

Tanner sipped his hot chocolate and cleared his throat. "Yeah, your abilities—they are definitely something to talk about. I've noticed how much more powerful you're becoming. Even in class, you are better at magic than Peter or Kathleen. You don't let people know it, though. I think I like that the best."

Alison smiled and licked some whipped cream off her finger. "I just don't like to be a showboat. As a Drow, I have to be careful with my magic. Unfortunately, I don't have another Drow around to tell me what's right or wrong. I just have to kinda figure it out on my own."

Tanner squeezed her hand and looked at the other magical beings walking up and down the street. He stared at a Kilomea for several seconds, watching him lurch along stomping his large feet on the pavement, his face twisted into a frown.

"I can't imagine what that would be like, having all

these powers but not really knowing what they are. Mine are pretty cut and dried, but yours… They aren't even in any books, really."

Alison nodded. "I know. I've read just about every book in the library by this point, and I've found very little information."

Tanner took a deep breath and stared at Alison, thinking about how beautiful she was. "I did some research of my own while I was on vacation since I wanted to try to help you, but you're right. There's not much information out there. You are pretty tough, though. I like that about you."

Alison giggled, and her cheeks burned. "Thanks, though I have to say I might not be so likable when I accidentally blow someone up or drop them from a building."

Tanner chuckled. "Remind me not to go on top of any tall buildings with you in the future."

They both laughed, leaning back in their chairs and enjoying their time together. The kemana turned out to be the perfect place to finish their date, and neither Alison nor Tanner was thinking the least bit about Jason and what had happened back in town. Tanner was right, though. Alison's powers were strong, and she was barely starting to get the slightest hint of exactly how strong they were.

"I hope you had a good time," Tanner said as the two walked up the steps back into the school.

Alison nodded and smiled. "Probably the best time I've

had at the school so far. The hot chocolate was pretty awesome."

Tanner laughed, and Alison giggled. "I'll have to remember that. Bring hot chocolate on every date with Alison, so she has a good time. Check."

Tanner walked beside Alison up the staircase to the third level and down the hall. They held hands but were quiet, knowing there were probably people trying to sleep or study. When they reached her door, they could hear the girls giggling inside and talking about whatever. Alison turned toward Tanner, holding both his hands in front of her and took a deep breath.

"Well, this is where it ends. At least this date."

Tanner squeezed her hands. "Thanks for going out with me and getting to know me better. We need to do this on a regular basis."

Alison nodded, smirking at the laughter inside. "I agree with you. I love my friends, but having alone time was definitely worth it."

They stood there for a moment quietly until Tanner put his hand on her cheek and pressed his lips softly to hers. Alison lifted onto her tiptoes and closed her eyes, feeling the energy rushing between them. They held that for a moment until Tanner pulled away and smiled, brushing his hand one last time across her cheek.

He kissed her forehead, whispering, "Good night. I'll see you in the morning."

Alison nodded. Butterflies fluttered through her stomach and chest. She smiled and watched his energy go back down the hall and turn the corner. She leaned against the door, letting the moment simmer inside her. She wasn't ready to let it go.

Alison was over the moon about the kiss and about Tanner. She couldn't remember another time in her life when she had felt like that.

"Look, I know it's a special day and that the veil is thin, but that doesn't mean that you need to go messing around with it," a dark wizard senior said to his younger sister.

She rolled her eyes and crossed her arms. "I'm a dark witch just like you're a dark wizard. And I'm in my second year, so I should be able to do whatever I want to. Can you imagine how proud mom and dad would be of me if I was able to talk to people beyond the veil in just my second year?"

The boy shook his head and grabbed his sister by the shoulders. "Just because you're a dark witch doesn't mean that messing with dark things is safe. Mom and Dad would be a lot prouder if you graduated than if you got sucked into the World in Between because you did something you didn't fully understand."

The girl sighed and nodded. "I was just gonna do a small spell."

"Don't mess with that! Uncle Fred is not a guy you want to talk to."

"I still don't understand how you're a dark wizard when you're so cautious and careful with everything," his sister said as she pulled away and walked down the hallway, still not understanding the danger.

The World in Between was a place many feared and few had seen and survived, and a place that made Alison curious. She wasn't steeped in its lore, but had learned several things about it just from being around the magical community. The headmistress was rumored to have spent years in the World in Between, but with the help of her granddaughter Leira she had escaped.

From what Alison understood, the World in Between held souls or people who either accidentally fell through a rift in a portal or had unfinished business. Either way, sometimes people—on certain occasions—could possibly be able to contact the dead. This alone sparked her interest, since her mother was deceased. She didn't have the repulsion that even the dark families had toward that place of mystery.

"I'll see you at dinner," Izzie whispered, shutting her book and patting Alison on the hand.

Alison nodded and smiled, glancing at the librarian and watching as Izzie's energy disappeared out the doors and around the corner. There was no one else in the library since it was early evening and people were either eating dinner or in their rooms studying. Alison, however, had found a book that introduced her to spells that might allow her to contact someone in the World in Between.

"Will you be all right for a moment? I'm going to go into the stacks and make sure everything is organized correctly," the librarian asked, tapping Alison on the shoulder.

Alison covered the book and her braille reader with one of her textbooks and smiled up at Librarian Decker. "Of course. I'm just doing some light reading. I wasn't really feeling like dinner tonight."

"I might go get a snack before I start, but if anybody comes in you remind them not to take any books out without me here."

Alison giggled. "Of course."

The librarian's energy shimmered and swirled as he made his way out of the library, closing the door behind him. Alison quickly uncovered the book and slid the braille reader back over the text. She read through the spell just one more time to make sure she had everything right. It seemed like a simple-enough spell. She really hoped she could contact her mother through it, or maybe someone else in her family.

Alison took a deep breath and stood up, keeping her fingers pressed tightly against the reader to make sure she got all the words correct. She had heard about so many spells going wrong, and the last thing she wanted to do was get sucked into the World in Between because she messed around with something she didn't understand.

Alison felt the magic flowing through her, the warmth of it heating up every part of her body. She closed her eyes, rolled her neck from side to side, and ran her fingers over the words a final time. When she was ready she opened her eyes, but in place of her normally bright-blue pupils, there was nothing but a stormy gray.

Alison whispered the spell, *"Those who have passed the wavering line, sinking deep between the vine. An endless wake and thoughtless stumble leave those in between tired and bumbled. Through this spell, I call to thee, my loved ones close, show yourselves to me."*

In reality, Alison just wanted to learn more. She wanted to talk to someone who could explain to her who she was, and she really wanted to understand this crazy other dimension that people talked about and feared so much. She didn't actually think the spell would work, especially since she had no idea what she was doing. However, as she finished the words to the spell, the table beneath her began to shake, and she felt the magic circling through her body and going out through her palms.

She shook her head, trying to see the energy that was swirling around her, but all she could see were the dark rays that shot from her hands. Alison stepped back, knocking over the chair behind her, and closed her hands, just wanting it all to stop. She heard a low growl, and it made the hairs on the back of her neck stand up.

Alison shook her head in disbelief. "No, I take it back. Stop the spell. I didn't mean to."

It was too late, though. The spell had been cast, and as Alison stood there in the center of the library, a tear ripped the air in front of her. She watched in horror as the dead began to climb out. At first, she thought that they would pull her in, but then she saw that they were just escaping from where they were. They clawed their way out of the portal and rushed for the doors of the library.

Alison didn't wait for the tear to close, just turned and ran for the door. She didn't know how to stop it, and the energy just kept coming. She raced down the hallway toward the cafeteria. She needed her friends' help, and although she didn't know if they had any idea what to do, she couldn't face this alone.

Alison skidded to a halt at their table, glancing up to make sure the headmistress wasn't watching. "I need your help, all of you."

Ethan was in midsentence, but he stopped talking, looking up at Alison's frightened face. "What's going on?"

Izzie turned in her chair and grabbed Alison's hand. "What is it? You look like you've seen a ghost."

Alison raised an eyebrow and let out a deep breath. "I think that might be understating the situation. Please, just come with me, and I'll show you. We have to do something."

Everyone nodded and glanced at the professors onstage, glad to see that they weren't paying attention to them. Izzie took Alison by the hand as they walked out of the cafeteria and down toward the library. As they approached the door they looked around them, seeing spirits floating down the corridor.

Ethan poked his hand through one of the ghosts and laughed. "That's an interesting spell, and it's not even Halloween yet."

Alison shivered and shook her head. "That's not even the half of it. And trust me, they aren't some figment of your imagination."

Ethan looked at her strangely, but Alison just opened the library door and ushered her friends in. As soon as they stepped inside and shut the door behind them they gasped, watching as the spirits climbed out of the tear and left the library. They didn't even need to open the doors to leave, just floated right through them.

Kathleen put her hand over her mouth and looked at the others wide-eyed. "This is bad. Not because of the energy necessarily, but because anything can come through that tear. From what I've heard, there are some really nasty things in the World in Between."

Aya grabbed Alison's wrist. "Did you do this? Did you open a tear to the World in Between?"

Alison rubbed her forehead, grabbed the back of the closest chair, and plopped down. "I was just curious. I didn't know this would happen. I thought that maybe I could contact someone I knew, and they would come and visit me. I didn't know I would open an entire tear to the World in Between and let a bunch of dead people out. Either way, Kathleen is right. This is really bad. I need you guys to help me figure out how to get all these spirits back."

The tear snapped shut, and the remaining spirits floated out of the library. The group gathered at one of the tables and sat down. They looked up as the door opened, and the librarian walked in. He shook his head and dusted off his shirt. "Someone's in the Halloween spirit early."

The group smiled nervously and waited until he moved to the back before leaning forward and whispering to each other.

Izzie realized that none of them found humor in the librarian's words. Peter looked like he was about to pass out. "Okay, I know there's a book somewhere in this library that can help us come up with a way to get the spirits back where they belong."

Alison dropped the book in the middle of the table. "I think this is what you're looking for, but I can't understand most of it."

Izzie flipped through the pages, reading as fast as she could. The others kept watch to make sure Librarian Decker didn't sneak up on them and find out what they were doing.

Izzie put the open book down and pointed her finger at the page. "This is it. We need to corral the spirits somewhere that people aren't going to notice, then we light four blue candles one at a time, saying the incantation."

Emma grabbed her bag and stood up. "I have four blue candles in the room. I had them for some project, and I figured I'd keep them in the room for a calming atmosphere. Where do you guys want to meet?"

Peter swallowed hard and rubbed his face. "Probably the garden with the big tree beside the school. You know, the one that's right on the edge with the commemorative bench for one of the professors who passed away. That's probably the best spot. No one will notice us out there."

Ethan slapped Peter on the back. "Good thinking. Is there something we can use to gather the spirits in one place?"

Kathleen nodded. "Yeah, my mom told me about an incantation from some séance she went to. Apparently, if you say it over and over—it's in Latin—it will draw the spirits to us."

Emma went to grab the candles while the others

collected their things and made their way out to the gardens. It was getting dark, and most of the students had gone to their rooms for the night, so there was no one there to bother them. Even next to the school though, under the wavering limbs of the willow tree, an eerie feeling had fallen over all of them.

They stood in a circle. Ethan took the Aya's and Peter's hand on either side of him. "Okay, Kathleen, what's the incantation?"

Kathleen took a deep breath and took Peter and Alison's hands. "*Spiritibus venit ad me iungere mihi hic locus.*"

Kathleen said it again and again, slowly at first so everyone could understand, then picked up speed as the others repeated the chant. After about five minutes, Emma came through the path and put the four candles down in the center of their circle. She joined hands with the others and began repeating Kathleen's incantation.

Ethan looked around with wide eyes. "It's working. They're coming."

The spirits swirled around them, their moans and groans filling their ears. Izzie began lighting the candles as she whispered the spell from the book. The ground trembled slightly, and everyone gripped each other's hands tighter. However, as the light of the flames flickered and shimmered, the spirits screamed in anger, dipping back and forth, left and right, and jetting off into the grounds.

Aya dropped their hands in frustration and shook her head. "They seem to know what you're trying to do. We drew them in, that worked, but when you try to open the tear to push them back through, it's like they know the words."

Alison bit her lip and thought for a moment, figuring anything was worth trying at that point. "What if we gather them, then I do the same spell I used to open it only this time we coax them into the tear somehow. There's a pull to it, so I know if they get close it might work."

Kathleen shrugged. "It's worth a try, I guess."

They blew out the candles, and everyone chanted in Latin again to gather the spirits.

"*Spiritibus venit ad me iungere mihi hic locus.*"

Spirits reappeared but only half of them, swirling and whizzing by the group as they shouted. Alison reached down and grabbed the book, placing her braille reader over it and running her fingers over the spell again. Before she could start it, one of the larger spirits swooped down and slammed the book shut in her hands, knocking it to the ground before all of them took off back into the grounds again.

Everyone dropped hands and looked at each other, not knowing what to do at that point. Izzie wrapped her arms around Alison and hugged her, knowing she was upset. Kathleen tapped her chin, thinking about what to do next.

Ethan looked at the others. "We can't give up. We need to do some more research, but we're going to have to be stealthy about it since the librarian is still in there."

Peter scoffed. "Yeah, and also try not to get sucked into the World in Between while we're trying to figure out how to get these apparitions back where they belong."

Emma kept a positive tone, picking up the candles and putting them in her bag. "Look, guys, if there's a spell to open it, then there's a way to close it and get everyone back in. We just have to figure out what that is. Not all of them even have to go back in. Some of them can just cross over."

Aya crossed her arms, looking nervous. "Yeah, but how do we do *that*? We don't know the advanced spells and even people like Izzie and Alison who have stronger magic don't know what to do to fix this."

Emma shrugged, putting one hand on Alison's. "I don't know, but we have to do something… Well, *anything* to fix this. Otherwise, Alison is facing serious trouble from the headmistress, and who knows what kind of problems letting those spirits out could create. We've faced tougher things. Together, we can do this."

Everyone headed back into the courtyard. A group of students was talking next to the picnic tables.

"Dude, did you see the dead guy that was missing the eyeball? Whoever made that magic trick is pretty sick. They shoulda waited for Halloween, though. It would've been awesome walking the halls with them."

Ethan lifted an eyebrow and looked at Peter. "Yeah, except they don't realize that they're walking around with the walking dead."

The whole group went to the library, ignoring the strange looks from the librarian. They skimmed through several books, reading quietly and trying to ignore the spirits that swooped in and out of the library periodically. After about an hour, Emma stood up and rushed over to the others, opening the book and pointing down at something.

Izzie read through it. "This seems like it could work. Basically, we say the spell whenever we're near a spirit, and it should push them back to wherever they came from. We can split up and get them all back quicker that way."

"I'm down," Ethan said, nodding .

"Let's do this," Emma replied, standing next to Kathleen.

Aya and Alison nodded, and they all took off. Izzie paired up with Luke. The two of them ran through the hallways, chasing a rather large spirit into the back closets where they kept old textbooks and such. Izzie put up her hands as she slowly backed the spirit into the corner.

"Come on, buddy. This isn't the place for you," she said, letting two balls of light form in her palms.

The soul tilted its wavering head toward her and narrowed its eyes, and the black mist around its ankle swirled toward Izzie. She took a step back as the soul grew larger and its eyes began to glow a deep crimson. Izzie shook her head at the soul, but before she could release the energy in her hands, Luke jumped in front of her. His eyes were bright yellow, and his teeth had transformed into jagged sharp edges. He let out a deep growl, pushing the soul backward.

Luke turned his glowing eyes toward Izzie. "Do the spell!"

Izzie nodded and put her hands backed out. "*From dark, you came to light, and back you shall go, where you belong, only you know.*"

Lights exploded from her palms and across the floor, creating two orbs behind the spirit. Suddenly, two tears ripped through the air behind him, and large, taloned hands reached out. The spirit attempted to get away, but the hands pulled him backward until he disappeared in a bright flash of light. Izzie lowered her hands, and Luke stepped beside her.

Izzie chuckled and shook the remaining magic from her fingertips. "It worked."

Luke nodded, letting his sharp teeth recede and his eyes dim again. "Sorry I jumped in like that. I saw you in trouble, and I couldn't help myself."

Izzie kissed him on the cheek. "I liked it. Come on, let's go get the rest of them."

All across the campus and throughout the grounds, the group pushed the spirits back to where they came from. Alison and Aya stood at the edge of the forest. Both held their hands out, cornering one of the last spirits. Alison could see the dark and light fighting each other inside the soul, and though it didn't want to go back, Alison didn't get the feeling that the spirit was all bad.

The soul whipped streams of magic toward Alison and Aya and they ducked, letting the magic dissipate into the air behind them. At that point the others approached, Kathleen and Emma looked proud but worried. Peter and Ethan dusted the dirt and mud off their pants from whatever they had gotten into, and Izzie and Luke held hands as they moved toward them.

The woman put her hands up and shook her head, the remnants of her long blonde hair shimmering translucent in the wind. "Please, I don't mean you any harm. I got out with the rest of them, but I need to get a message to a student here."

Izzie touched Alison's wrist. "Who is the student?"

"Misty, Misty Albertson. She was my niece, and I need her to know that I'm okay. My death was tragic, an accident that none of us ever saw coming. My home caught fire in the middle of the night, and the smoke overtook me before I could get out of my bed. I perished in the fire, but Misty got out okay. I need her to know that we are okay now, her uncle and me. I've been waiting so long to get that message out."

Alison eased her stance and nodded, seeing the dark slip away from the energy and leaving nothing but light flowing through her. It was obvious to Alison that whoever this was, that she'd been light energy when she walked the earth. "We'll tell her. We promise."

The woman smiled as a tear ripped in the air behind her revealing only light and calmness. "Tell her the strength of the butterfly is still within her. She'll know what I mean." She walked toward it, relieved of her duty and was absorbed into the light.

Alison, Izzie, Luke, Emma, Kathleen, Ethan, Peter, and Aya all held hands as they watched the dead woman fade into the light. When the rift shut, it released a large bolt of energy that blew them backward and onto the ground. As the light circled them, they were shown a message of who was really behind everything that happened.

The light faded, and everyone climbed to their feet, they all looked at each other in amazement. Emma shook her head surprised. "It wasn't Alison. I mean, it was because Alison was screwing around with magic, but the real reason the darkness got in so easily was because of the dark forces that want to break up our school!"

"We need to find Misty Albertson right away," said Izzie.

Kathleen nodded, "I think she's in our dorm. Quiet girl, and now, I guess we know why." She rubbed her head. "You saw it too?"

"How could you miss it?" muttered Emma in amazement. She glanced at Peter and Ethan, who were still staring at the place where the woman faded away. Kathleen looked at Izzie. "What about you? And Luke?"

Izzie smiled and took Luke's hand. "I saw it. There're dark forces trying to get in here."

Luke shook the bright yellow from his eyes and glanced down at Izzie. "I saw it too…the whole thing."

Alison took Izzie's hand and looked at Peter, who already knew what they were thinking. He clasped his hands together nervously. He felt terrible for not telling them from the beginning, but he knew he had to find out more information before he could let everyone in on it.

Izzie put her hand on Peter's shoulder and nodded. "You need to tell the others."

The rest of the group looked at him suspiciously and waited for him to speak. Peter took a deep breath and cleared his throat, glancing at all of them. "It all started when I went to do a story about the lines being painted in the parking lot. I heard three dark wizards talking about taking over the school. I decided to do more research on it and figure out what was really going on. Izzie and Alison know about that part because I ran into them that night when I was out looking for the wizards by the fence. But there's more…"

They looked at each other with fear and anger, waiting

for Peter, who was trying to put his thoughts together. He licked his lips and tapped his hands against his sides. "The dark forces, wizards from the different dark families—they want to close the school down."

Kathleen shook her head confused. "Why? They just started sending their own kids here."

Peter shook his head. "I know. I don't think it's those families that are involved, but I don't know for sure. What I *do* know is that these dark forces don't just want to close the school because light magic is here. They want to do it so they can control magic in general."

Ethan clenched his fists and looked at Luke, who was just as angry. "Who the hell do they think they are? Do they really think we would allow that?"

Peter stepped back to get a better view of everyone. "That's not all. They're looking for a girl, a student who goes to our school. In fact, they seem to be hunting her."

Izzie and Alison both swallowed hard. Each wondered if she was the one being hunted. Izzie quickly got control of her emotions and looked at Peter. "Well, who is she? I mean, did they say? If they did, we have to get her to safety. We have to tell the headmistress who she is, because if they're hunting her, there's something very special about her. Something we aren't going to want to let fall into the hands of the dark wizards, especially if there trying to take over magic."

Ethan put his hands in his pockets and looked down at the ground. "I guess it makes sense then that they're trying to take over the school. Whoever this is must be the key to them controlling magic."

Peter nodded at Ethan then looked at Izzie, shrugging.

"They never said what her name was. It almost felt like they didn't know it, or at least not all of them. I don't know. That's all I've found out so far."

Alison shook her head, scanning at Peter's energy. "I don't understand. The last time we talked to you about this, all you knew was that they had something planned for the shifters. How did you get so much more information?"

Ethan crossed his arms over his chest. "Yeah, how *did* you get so much information? Does this have anything to do with you going to newspaper meetings that I know haven't been happening? I've stopped by, and there was no newspaper meeting when you claimed there was."

Peter grimaced not wanting to let on to what he'd been doing. He knew the guys would be angry. "Look, I didn't want anybody else to be involved, and I didn't want anybody else's life to be in danger. We have no idea who this girl they are searching for is."

"Why didn't you tell a teacher?"

"After the toombie," he said, glancing up at Alison, "I wanted to be sure of who all the players were before I said anything. That girl could be anyone. A friend, maybe. So, I went out on my own, sneaking off-campus and going to different shady bars in town. I glamoured myself to look older and covered myself in robes to eavesdrop on the dark wizards in town. It's amazing how many of them are parked here, just sitting out in broad daylight talking about doing badassery evil doings."

Luke stepped up next to Ethan and crossed his arms, frowning. "I think that's pretty stupid of you, Peter. You went out there by yourself, and you could have easily been found out. What would you have done if the dark wizards had found out you were spying on them? None of us have enough power to defend ourselves against that, except maybe Izzie and Alison."

Izzie nodded, disappointed in Peter. "I agree, and even Alison and I can't always control our magic. It's too new to us."

Ethan could tell Peter felt bad, and he walked over and put his hand on the boy's shoulder. "Look, man, we're not trying to make you feel bad. You got some incredible information, and I'm pretty impressed. The thing is, we don't want anything to happen to you. That's why we always stick together. We're a team here, and we stand up for each other. If something is going on, don't worry about whether you have enough information. Just come to us, and we can help you find the information if it's out there. Three or five or however many light magical beings facing down dark wizards is a lot better than one school-aged kid who half the time blows himself up with magic."

Emma smiled gently at Peter. "He's right, Peter. It's like the kemana in our first year or the townies last year who wanted to attack us. We worked together and were able to defeat them. Even if some of us are more powerful than others, we all need each other in some way, shape, or form. You should've trusted us. By now, you should realize that we won't let you down."

Kathleen nodded and gave him her best smile. "We've got each other's backs, and don't forget that again. We don't want anything to happen to you, especially if we could've prevented it by being there."

Peter nodded and looked at the others in the group, understanding what they were saying. "Well, I hope it's not too late now because I could really use your help. We need to get to the bottom of this for so many reasons. Quite honestly, the future of magicals depends on it, at least light magic. We know how these families work. They're not just going to let light magical beings go walking around if they're in control. On top of that, I want to put this in the school newspaper. It will be my first breaking story, and something I could really be proud of."

Everyone started talking at once.

"You didn't even use magic to dig this up, did you?" asked Emma in amazement. "Old school, I like it."

Ethan laughed and slapped him on the back. "You'll win some kind of award if you crack this."

Luke pointed at them with raised eyebrows. "And saved the school…"

Kathleen rolled her eyes. "Or get us all kicked out or killed."

Aya smirked at him. "Yeah, but don't forget that you're supposed to be writing about Professor Fowler's herb garden. Forgetting that is one quick way to get us caught."

Peter tilted his head back and rolled his eyes, clenching his fists. He groaned loudly, and everyone else laughed, patting him on the shoulder as they made their way back toward the school.

"Hey, isn't that Misty Albertson? That's the girl…" Kathleen's voice trailed away.

A girl with a long braid and brown glasses was walking down the sidewalk by herself, avoiding eye contact.

"We never found her," muttered Aya, "with everything that was going on."

"No time like the present," said Peter, emboldened. "She deserves to know."

"You're a force, dude," said Luke, smiling.

Kathleen waved to the girl and called, "Misty? Misty! Hey, aren't we in the same gym class?" She fell into step beside her. "Boy, do we have a story for you!"

Misty looked confused and pulled her books closer to her chest. "Do we… I mean…"

"We don't know you yet, but we *have* met your aunt."

Misty's eyes grew wide and the color drained from her face. "That's impossible," she stammered.

"At this school, the list of impossible grows shorter every day. Maybe we should start from the beginning. My name's Kathleen, and there was this thin place between here," she said, sweeping her arm around, "and the World in Between."

"She's in the World in Between?" Misty's look of shock was only growing.

"Cut to the chase," urged Luke, then pressed his lips together.

"Yeah, we can fill in the background later. I'm Peter." Peter held out his hand and Misty reluctantly shook it, immediately letting go.

"Fine, sure. Geez, this isn't easy."

"How about, we kind of tore a hole open for a second and talked to your aunt. She said to tell you she's glad you got out okay and to stop worrying. She's okay."

"We even saw her cross over and become part of the light," shrugged Luke.

Misty wrinkled her nose and hunched her shoulders. "Look, I don't know why you guys are doing this, but I don't appreciate it."

"She doesn't believe us." Aya chewed her bottom lip as Misty sped up, trying to put some distance between her and the small group.

"Wait! She said to tell you that you still have the strength of the butterfly within you. Said you'd know what that meant."

Misty froze where she was and a long, deep breath escaped her, like she had been holding it in forever. Her shoulders dropped, and her eyes shone with tears. "You *did* see her," she gasped.

Emma caught up to her and gently put her arm around the girl's shoulders, squeezing them. "She just wants you to be happy."

"My family are all Wood Elves. We change our looks constantly. My aunt always said that made us eternal butterflies who could do amazing things."

"I like it. Hey, we're on our way to the celebration. Come with us."

"That's the least we can do," muttered Luke, and Kathleen elbowed him.

"A Wood Elf, huh? Very cool," mused Peter. "You must be able to go wherever you want without being seen. Ever think of being on the school newspaper?"

"Thanks for meeting me out here," Peter said, standing in front of Alison and Izzie on one of their late-night strolls.

Alison smiled. "Of course. We said we'd be here for you. Besides, I didn't even think about asking Dorvu for help. He's all over the grounds all the time. If there's an intruder, he will be up for finding them."

Peter looked out over the rolling hills that adjoined the forest. "Yeah, but how are you supposed to find him?"

Izzie nodded in the direction of the forest. "It's night-time, which means he'll be out hunting his dinner."

Peter walked nervously behind them, still not used to being around the dragon. As they reached the edge of the woods, they stopped. Izzie cupped her hands around her mouth.

"Dorvu! Dorvu, we need you!"

They immediately heard a rustle in the treetops and the sound of the dragon's wings clipping through the branches as he made his way to their voices. When he landed he let out a cold snort, icing the ground around him. He threw his head back and crunched down on the last of whatever furry animal he had been eating, then looked at the girls and Peter.

"I was just thinking about you while I was hunting my dinner," Dorvu said through fur covered teeth.

Peter grimaced and looked the other way while Izzie laughed and walked forward to pat Dorvu on the head. "You've grown quite a bit. But that's not why we came. We need your help with something. There are people who are trying to take over the school, and we know that they're close to the boundaries."

Dorvu growled. "I'll tear apart anyone that tries to harm my family."

Alison walked over and patted Dorvu. "That may not be necessary. If we can figure out where they are, we can get the professors to take care of them. We are gonna walk the fence, but we need you overhead keeping an eye out."

Dorvu began to flap his wings. "Of course. I like a little recon late in the evening."

The girls laughed and made their way across the field to the fence while Peter walked behind them, gawking at the dragon flying overhead. They walked for what seemed like miles, carefully inching along the fence, but they didn't see anything. Among all the trees, vines, and weeds, there was no one except the faeries and other magical beings.

Izzie sighed and stopped at the edge of the forest. "I don't think they're out here. Not tonight, at least."

Peter nodded. "I agree. I haven't seen them again since I found them in the parking lot that day. I guess I'd better head back, so I don't get in trouble. The dorm proctor likes to do a roving watch at night to make sure we're not sneaking out."

Alison nodded and stretched her arms over her head. "I'm going to stay out here for a little bit longer, I think. If nothing else, I'll enjoy the night air."

Izzie took a seat next to the fence and patted the ground, reaching up and grabbing Alison's hand. "I'll stay with you."

Peter backed up a bit as Dorvu landed next to them. "Okay, thanks for the help. See you in the morning."

Dorvu curled up in a semicircle, and the girls scooted over to him, surprised at how warm his body was considering everything else about him was cold. They leaned back against him and looked at the stars, wondering if they would find the wizards lurking around the property.

Dorvu yawned, and his scales shimmered in the moonlight with the movement. "I don't know about you ladies, but I want to get some sleep."

Izzie patted him and smiled. "I think I'm just gonna lie here for a while, then we'll go back."

The girls laid there for quite a while, just watching the stars shimmer. However, the warmth of the dragon combined with the time of night made them grow drowsy. Before they knew it, they were sleeping in the leaves, curled up with Dorvu. It was an interesting mix: a dragon, a Drow princess, and a Jasper Elf. They were the perfect combination to help the dragon grow, although they didn't know that.

As all three slept, Dorvu didn't notice that he started to grow from a medium-size youth to a full-sized dragon.

The early morning sun peeked over the horizon, sending streams of golden light through the forest canopy. Izzie grumbled and turned on her side, running her hand up what she thought was the mattress. However, when her hand skipped across Dorvu's cold scales, she slowly opened her eyes and looked around. Alison was dead asleep next to her and Dorvu. He'd grown by leaps and bounds overnight and was snoring gently.

It took Izzie a moment to realize what was going on, but when she did, she panicked. "Holy shit! Alison, wake up! It's morning, and we're still in the woods!"

Alison's eyes shot wide open and she sat up, taking in the energy around her. "Crap!"

Both the girls jumped up, picked the leaves off their pants quickly, and moved as quickly as they could through the woods, Izzie doing her best to guide Alison. They didn't even say goodbye to Dorvu, who had slept through their panic. As they reached the edge of the woods, they stopped and looked at the courtyard and let out a sigh of relief. No one had come outside quite yet, but that didn't mean they were in the clear.

"It has to be time for breakfast," Izzie said, shaking her head.

Alison nodded calmly. "Okay, we head to the side door by the garden, and we get up the stairs before anyone sees us. There should be enough people coming out of the dorms for us to just kind of sneak back in to change."

Izzie shrugged. "I guess there's no other option. Ready when you are."

They dashed across the green fields and through the courtyard, looking around with every pace to make sure no one saw them. They carefully opened the door, and Izzie looked right and left making sure no one was in the hallway yet. They scooted along the wall and came out in the main entry area, where they nonchalantly walked past a group of people going into the cafeteria, then ran up the stairs.

None of the girls barreling out of the dorm paid any attention to Alison or Izzie, so they were able to blend in with the students who were streaming out of the dorms. They made it to their dorm room, opening and closing the door quickly then leaned back against the dorm, breathing heavily just glad they got back there in one piece.

"Holy crap, that was close," Alison exclaimed.

"You're telling me. Everyone else is already at breakfast. We need to get changed and make it down there, so no one notices. When the girls ask… I don't know, we'll take it as it comes," Izzie said breathlessly as she ran over to change her clothes.

Outside the boys' dorm area and probably louder than they should've been, the boys were up to no good as usual.

One of the boys pulled the energy into his hand, creating a flame. "All right, boys and girls, and I emphasize *girls*, this is a face-off. Just like in the old Western days, you start face-to-face, turn and walk ten paces, and turn back, ready to fire. The first person who goes down is the loser, of course. Let's just try not to kill or maim anyone, or destroy the building."

The boys stood face-to-face, trying to give each other evil looks but unable to hold back their laughter. They shook hands and turned quickly, taking one step every time the boy called a number.

The boys smirked, juggling the fire in their hands with their backs toward each other. "On the count of three, turn. One, two…"

"What are you boys doing? You're supposed to be at breakfast," the dorm proctor yelled as he came around the corner.

The boys scrambled for their bookbags and ran for the stairs as fast as they could. Connor sighed, tired of dealing with the idiots. He chased them, but by the time he got to the top of the stairs they were gone. They hadn't *technically* done anything to get in trouble…yet.

He slapped his hand on the stair railing, and shook his head, turning back toward the dorms. "Great, they learned about face-offs. This is definitely going to get messy."

"The time is growing near, my little beautiful plants. The warm air and spring sunshine will bring you right out," Professor Lucy Fowler whispered as she tended the magical herb garden.

The plant swayed, listening attentively to everything she said. It was known that Oriceran plants did much better when you had full-on conversations with them. Some of them even attempted to communicate back, using unique motions to signal different things. Professor Fowler had been in the plant business for so long that she was fluent in plant speak.

"What's that?" Professor Fowler bent closer to the plants that were leaning toward her.

She giggled, and her cheeks turned red as she looked down at her dress as if the plants had given her a compliment. Just then a whoosh of wind blew around her, and she grabbed her hat, looking into the sky. Dorvu coasted overhead. His wingspan was much wider, and his scales shimmered silver in the sun. She narrowed her eyes, slightly taken back by how large he had gotten.

She looked at the plants waving in the breeze. "He's gotten big pretty fast, hasn't he? Curious. Very curious."

Professor Fowler gathered her things and stood up, dusting off her knees, then headed to the mansion to seek out the headmistress. Her hands were still covered in dirt and left smudges on the sides of her gardening dress as she walked. She nodded at one of the students as she knocked hard on the office door.

"Come in," the headmistress yelled.

Professor Fowler opened the ornate wooden door, then stepped inside and closed it behind her. When she turned around, the headmistress was closing a small box, She tapped it with her wand and smiled. "What can I do for you, Professor Fowler?"

The professor kept her hands clenched tightly, trying not sprinkle dirt on the floor. "I was out in the herb garden, and the silver dragon flew over."

The headmistress sat down in her chair and nodded. "That happens. He's been more active recently since the weather isn't as cold as it usually is."

The professor hesitated for a moment but then decided just to go for it. "He just seems to be growing so quickly. I was shocked by how large he is. You don't have any idea what might be making that happen, do you?"

The headmistress smiled and laid her hands on the desk in front of her. "I don't. Dragons are very interesting creatures. We don't have a lot of knowledge of them here on Earth. I do thank you for bringing it to my attention, though, and I will definitely look into it. I'm also looking forward to seeing the herbs this year. I hear your herb garden is a showstopper."

Professor Fowler giggled and stepped backward the door. "I sure hope it is. I've worked hard enough on it. Let me know if you need any help with the dragon."

Headmistress Berens waved at her, forcing a smile. "I will."

The headmistress waited until the door closed behind the professor and dropped her smile. Having spent so much time on Oriceran she knew quite a bit about dragons, and it wasn't rocket science for her to figure out what exactly had happened. She returned the box to the shelf and headed out of the room, locking the door behind her. The last few students lingering in the hallways ran off as soon as they saw her. They knew they'd be in trouble if they got caught after the second bell.

The headmistress headed to the library. She needed to get just a little bit more information, and knew exactly which book she wanted to look at. The girls didn't know, but it was a natural thing for a dragon to pull energy from those around it. It was obvious that the dragon had drawn energy from Izzie and Alison while he was still in his egg. What shocked the headmistress was that he continued to do so, which led her to believe that the dragon was still seeing them.

The headmistress pushed open the library door and looked up to find Leo standing on a stool, putting away some books. "Don't mind me. I just need to look up a couple of things."

The librarian raised his eyebrow and watched as the headmistress went through the shelves, pulling several books down and flipping through the pages. She walked over to the restricted section and waved her wand to unlock it. Leo casually walked over and stood just outside the fenced cage.

"I'm not spying on you, headmistress," Librarian Decker assured her.

Headmistress Berens chuckled and flipped through a very old book. "I know. No one, including me, is allowed to be in the restricted section alone. I promise I won't take too much of your time."

She ran her fingers down the paragraph on silver dragons and stopped when she found the line she knew was in that ancient book: Jasper energy was set free by silver dragons. It was a rare occurrence, but it could happen, and apparently, that was exactly what was happening to Izzie. That energy was zapping around her, not only wreaking havoc on her ability to control her magic but causing the memory spell to break down.

Mara shook her head and closed the book. "Not good. Not good at all."

"Class that is why gnomes wear that particular uniform, no matter where you see them," Professor Eleanor Hudson said to her class as the bell rang.

The students stood up and started to shuffle their bags, and Professor Hudson noticed the headmistress standing in the doorway, tapping her foot. It was obvious she had something important to talk to her about, but the professor needed to get her students out first.

"Okay, class, don't forget the homework due next week, and try to stay out of trouble," she called, winking at one of the students.

As the students exited, the headmistress entered the room, smiling kindly at them as they passed. She waited until the last had left and waved her hand, shutting the door and locking it. Professor Hudson closed her book and put it away in the drawer. She looked at the headmistress, lifted her brow, and walked over to meet her.

Professor Hudson studied the headmistress for a moment. "I haven't seen this much worry on you in a very long time. I have to say, I don't like it. What's going on?"

The headmistress took her by the hands, and the two sat down in seats across from each other. "I need your help, but first, I need to know that whatever I tell you will be kept strictly between you and me. It is a matter of life and death, and I'm not exaggerating."

Professor Hudson placed her hand on her chest and nodded. "Of course. You know that you can trust me. I would never put someone's life in danger."

Headmistress Berens let out a sigh. "I do know, and that's why I came to you. I can't tell you the whole story, not yet, but Izzie is in danger. I need to figure out how to protect her from something very dark. Something none of us have faced before. We are on the precipice of a possibly huge event, and Izzie stands in the center of it. I am the only one here to protect her now, and I gave my word—an oath on my life—that I would protect her from everything."

Professor Hudson took a deep breath and swallowed hard, looking down at her hands. "Izzie is a very talented and very powerful elf. I know she is a Jasper elf; that was not hard to figure out. Her biggest weakness is that she cannot control the light, a weakness she shares with many of her ancestors. If she can learn to do that, she'll be able to defeat any dark being, just like your granddaughter."

"I know. I just don't know how to protect her right now. There are a lot of things that you don't know, and a lot of things *she* doesn't know. It has to stay that way for now."

Professor Hudson nodded. "I understand."

The headmistress watched as she walked over to her desk and pulled out an ornate silver box. She drew a key hung from a chain around her neck, then held it to her lips and whispered something under her breath. Sparks of energy flew from her lips and twisted around the key. From the box, Professor Hudson extracted a silver bracelet with a sparkling green jewel in the center.

She glanced at the headmistress, then looked back down at the bracelet before closing the box and returning it to her desk drawer. She walked over and handed the bracelet to the headmistress. "Be careful with this. It has a lot of energy. A lot of *old* energy. It's from Oriceran, and it should protect Izzie, at least right now."

The headmistress wrapped the bracelet in a handkerchief she took from her pocket. She could feel the energy pulsing through it, and wondered if it would be too strong for Izzie. Then again, the same thing had been true of her granddaughter's bracelet, but on Leira, it did wonderful things.

Headmistress Berens looked at Professor Hudson. "Thank you so much for this, Eleanor. I won't forget the sacrifices that you have made for the school and for the students."

As the headmistress stood up, Professor Hudson touched her shoulder. "If you need anything—anything at all—you have only to ask. You know how loyal I am to the school and the students. If there is danger, I will be right beside you fighting it off. You know that. After all, I was once a Silver Griffin. I know that doesn't mean much to anyone now, but I believe it still counts for something. I have seen my fair share of dark days, and I know there are more to come, but don't ever think I've retired from fighting evil."

The headmistress smiled and squeezed her hand. "I know. You're one of my greatest allies here. And I promise, when the time comes that I can reveal the secrets, I will let you know. I know I can count on you to keep the students safe and to fight off the dark entities who are out there trying to hurt us. You don't know how important this bracelet is, and I hope it does something good for Izzie. She needs as much protection as possible right now."

The professor smiled and watched as the headmistress hurried from the room, leaving the door open behind her. Her smile faded, and she reached back in her blouse and clutched the key tightly in her hand. "I have a feeling that

Izzie isn't the only one who's going to be needing protection."

———

"How many of you have learned about or ridden the vast railway system made for the magical beings?" Professor Grant sat on the edge of her desk as she taught Hidden Earth's class.

Almost everybody in the class raised their hand. Most of them had already ridden it several times, especially coming back and forth to school every year. Professor Grant twisted her body and flicked her wand to pull down a map of the railway systems in front of the chalkboard.

"As you can see, class, the vast railway system can take you pretty much anywhere on Earth that you want to go. You can stop in all major cities. You can travel to all the different countries, and you can even request special stops in suburban areas. The railway is fast; faster than a car, a plane, or a boat. It is a technological and magical wonder—"

The headmistress stuck her head in the door, grabbing Professor Grant's attention. "I'm sorry to disturb you. May I please see Izzie for just a moment out here in the hall?"

The professor nodded and looked at Izzie, who abashedly got out of her chair and headed to the hallway, closing the door behind her. "Headmistress, is everything okay?"

The headmistress forced a smile and nodded, handing Izzie the bracelet. "I know you've been struggling with your energy and your spells. This bracelet is used to contain Jasper energy."

Izzie put the bracelet on her wrist and looked at the headmistress curiously. "What will it do?"

"It will help you control your growing powers, that's all. It'll make you a better student of the art of magic." The headmistress smiled.

"Thank you very much," Izzie said, about to take the bracelet off.

The headmistress clamped her hand around the bracelet, pushing it back on her wrist. "It's very important that you leave it on. It will only work if you never take it off. I know that sounds crazy, but please just trust me. This will really help you. You just have to have faith and keep it on."

Izzie looked at her strangely for a moment, then glanced at the bracelet, not really sure where this was coming from. But if it was going to help her control her magic and make her growing powers easier to control, she wasn't going to argue with the headmistress. "Okay, I promise I'll keep it on. Thank you for this. I was really hoping there was something out there that would help me. Alison has something too, though she has to take hers off."

The headmistress took her by the hands. "Izzie, I don't know how to explain this, but I just need you to trust me. Drow magic is different than yours. It is absolutely essential that you never take this off."

15

"You want to go get ice cream from the cafeteria with me?" Emma asked Izzie as she pulled her hoodie on.

Izzie smiled and grabbed her book off her bed. "I can't. I would love to, but the tryouts for *Beauty and the Beast* are today, and I don't want to be late. I heard there are a lot more people coming out to audition for this one."

"Oh, yeah, I completely blanked. Yeah, it's a popular one, for sure. Break a leg!"

Izzie waved at Emma as she left the dorm room and headed down the hall. There were several girls in front of her racing off to the auditorium for the auditions and talking excitedly about who they hoped to be cast as. Izzie didn't have a preference. She just hoped that she could do as well in this one as she did in *Wizard of Oz*, whatever her part.

Several of the girls ahead of her giggled as they passed the entrance to the gym. "Louper muscles for days!"

Izzie lifted an eyebrow as they continued past, then stopped and peeked around the gym door curious as to who they were talking about. —and blushed. She knew exactly what they were talking about. The entire Louper team was training inside, lifting weights and doing hurdles to gain as much strength and agility for the upcoming matches as they could.

As Izzie scanned the room, she saw Luke setting down one of the large weights. Sweat beaded his forehead, and he had a look of determination on his face. She touched her warm cheeks and giggled quietly, not wanting him to know she was spying. He was determined to become as strong and quick in real life as he could. All of a player's attributes, physical and mental, carried over into the game.

Izzie watched him for a couple of minutes, swooning on the inside at how strong he was getting. However, when someone giggled down the hall, Izzie realized she'd better be on her way before she missed the auditions. She wasn't sure if she would be disappointed by trading auditions for staring at her boyfriend and his muscles, though.

Izzie crept into the back of the auditorium. Scarlett and her gang were already there, standing up in the front rehearsing lines and warming up. She glanced at Izzie and smirked, flipping her hair over her shoulder.

"Look, little orphan Dorothy has arrived." She snickered. "Good luck."

For some reason, even though she was being catty, Izzie felt like her "good luck" might just be genuine, and the snark and attitude for show. She wouldn't put anything past Scarlett, but she had seen her true colors the year before—which had been true blue.

"Hey," Kathleen whispered as Izzie took a seat next to her.

"Hey. I didn't realize you would be here," Izzie replied.

Aya sat down next to Kathleen. "We couldn't miss a chance to be in this one. It's too good of a story."

"I agree." Izzie smiled.

Professor Fowler was once again directing the play, and climbed up onto the stage wearing a pair of flowing purple pants, a tight red turtleneck, and another hand-knitted vest with the word Director embroidered on the back. Her frizzy bright red hair was pulled halfway back, and she wore the same beret as the year before. She cleared her throat and held up her hand.

"Another year, another amazing play," she began dramatically. "So many new faces here. I just love it."

The professor floated her clipboard into her hands, flipped through the pages, and ran her finger down one, stopping on a name. "Let's get this show on the road, shall we? First up for auditions is Mary Beth Livingston."

Mary Beth, a sophomore with her blonde curls piled on top of her head, stood up nervously. She took the stage and waited for the professor to climb down and take a seat in the audience. The lights flickered and then dimmed. Peter and David manned the control booth. She cleared her throat and began the scene, deciding to go with the kidnapping of her father.

"Please, take me. Don't take him," she cried.

Everyone watched quietly except Scarlett and her friends, who whispered in the front row. Mary Beth pranced across the stage and slid down, holding her knees to her chest as if she were being locked away. That was where she ended the scene and stood to do the singing portion of her audition. She was okay but didn't knock anyone's socks off.

Professor Fowler stood up and smiled. "Thank you. Next, we have Eleanor Heady."

"She's a senior and always wanted to audition, but didn't because Scarlett scared her," Kathleen whispered to Izzie.

"What made her come out this year?" Izzie asked.

"You. Your bravery in standing up to Scarlett and winning last year."

Izzie raised her eyebrows and turned her attention back to the girl. She danced around the stage, singing with everything she had. Her voice filled the entire theater. She was good. Not polished, but definitely worth keeping an eye on. Izzie wished she had come out years before. If she had, by this point she would have blown everyone away.

The professor stood up when Eleanor was finished and smiled brightly. "Very nice. Thank you, Eleanor. Up next is Izzie, our star from last year."

Kathleen squeaked and patted her leg. "Good luck."

Izzie quietly walked down the aisle, ignoring Scarlett and her friends' stares as she climbed up on the stage and stood tall. "I'm going to start with *Beauty & The Beast* as my singing audition."

Professor Fowler nodded.

Izzie swallowed and looked up into the bright lights.

"Tale as old as time

True as it can be..."

Izzie sang her heart out, and by the end, the others were on their feet giving her a standing ovation. She did fantastically, but she really hoped she hadn't outdone her friends.

She wasn't expecting to be the lead, but she definitely wanted to be involved.

Professor Fowler waited until everyone had calmed down and stood up, clapping. "That was beautiful, Izzie. Thank you. Next up is Scarlett."

As Izzie descended the stairs, Scarlett stalked up to her, giving her a sly wink. Izzie smirked and continued back to her seat, smiling excitedly at Kathleen and Aya as Scarlett began her audition. She was ready that year; ready to get the main part, just like everyone else. She chose the opening scene, where Belle sang as she walked through the village, and Izzie had to admit that she did a really good job.

Scarlett walked across the stage dreamily with a book pressed to her chest.

"This is where she meets Prince Charming,
But she won't discover that it's him 'til Chapter Three."

Kathleen leaned over to Izzie. "Wow. Looks like the Good Witch washed off on her last year."

Izzie giggled and sat back in her seat, watching Scarlett until she finished. She was really good this year. When Kathleen took the stage, Izzie realized that she was up against some tough cookies. She was starting to think that Aya had the right idea by going into lighting instead of auditioning for the actual play. Then again, Izzie knew Aya just wanted to be near Peter even if she wouldn't admit it.

There was a lot of that going around that year, including David, who worked in lighting again with Peter. He was a very gifted Light Elf, and he knew how to enhance the lighting perfectly to make the play a success.

He had a crush on Scarlett, but like so many other people, she never even noticed him.

Kathleen sat back down in her chair and smiled at Izzie. "This is going to be one hell of a play."

Izzie couldn't agree more.

16

"I am so excited. I have been waiting for this game since the school year started," Tanner said as the group walked toward the Louper Stadium behind the school.

Alison smiled and slid her hand into his. "I know. You've only talked about it every day since the beginning of school."

They both laughed and entered the stands, taking the same seats they'd sat in the year before. Peter came in next to Emma, with Aya and Kathleen trailing behind. Aya looked like a lovesick puppy, but Kathleen was too busy thinking about the auditions to notice. They were all dressed in Cardinal t-shirts, and Izzie had magically put Luke's name on the back of hers.

Kathleen stopped at the edge of the seats and looked back at Izzie. "You coming?"

Izzie nodded and waved her hand. "I'll be there in just a second. Save me a seat!"

"Well, what do we have here? A beautiful young elf wandering behind the bleachers by herself?"

Izzie turned quickly, gasping, then laughed. Luke, dressed in his uniform, was leaning against one of the poles. "I like to be in dangerous situations."

Luke laughed and grabbed her by the wrist, pulling her close. "I've heard shifters are pretty dangerous."

Izzie feigned worry. "Oh, no! I was supposed to meet a handsome shifter behind the stands. Whatever shall I do?"

Luke smiled and kissed her. "I'll protect you."

Izzie kissed him again, then pulled back and put her hands on his chest. "Be careful out there. I know it's virtual, but I saw how everyone got hurt last year. This is a huge one. It's your first game of the season, and there are two matches back-to-back. You're gonna be exhausted by the second one."

Luke scoffed. "I've been working out. I got this."

Izzie rolled her eyes and smiled, slapping him on the arm. "Okay, big guy, get going. Your team is waiting for you. And good luck!"

Luke smiled as he headed toward the team on the other end of the bleachers, and Izzie just stood there until he disappeared. She made her way back to the entrance to the stands and climbed up, sitting next to Kathleen and Alison. The whole school had turned out for the event, so it was like a sea of red shirts. The only other color was the green of the playing field and the flag on the other side indicating the team that they played first—the New Orleans Crawfish.

Kathleen nudged Izzie. "Is he ready? It's the first game of the season."

Izzie lifted an eyebrow at her. "How did you know I just saw him?"

Kathleen scoffed. "Please. You have 'I just kissed my boyfriend' written all over your face."

Izzie put her hand on her cheek and giggled as the referee took the field. Everyone in the stands shushed each other until quiet fell over the stadium. The referee outlined the rules. Once completed, he introduced the opposition, letting the crowd see them for just a moment.

The crowd booed as the referee introduced them. "The New Orleans Crawfish are playing our very own SNM Cardinals!"

The crowd cheered as the Cardinals took the field and the team waved at the stands and lined up on the side, readying themselves for the game. The referee put his wand is straight up in the air, and the other team disappeared. He swirled it over his head and fired a shot of green energy straight up, and stepped back as it sprinkled over the players' heads. The team closed their eyes and waited for the magic to take hold.

Wyatt slapped Luke in the chest, making his eyes pop open. "You still with us, Luke?"

Luke found himself on the streets of Chicago. "I'm here. Let's do this."

Wyatt looked at the others. "We are breaking into three groups, one headed by me, one by Henry, and one by Luke. Listen to your team leaders and get to the treasure as fast as possible. Let's get a good start to the year."

All the players put their hands in the center and roared their battle cry, then took off in three different directions. Henry and his team started down the steps into the subways, finding a broken-down train at the platform. They jumped down to the tracks and moved through the tunnels. It was dark and dank, and water trickled down the walls as rats scuttled around their feet.

Henry put his finger to his lips when he heard something scratching along the walls ahead of them. Slowly, they crept forward, pulling out their wands and creating a light source. Their boots crunched on the gravel between the old tracks.

Henry squinted when he saw two small red circles, then jumped back as more began to glow in the darkness. "Spindles! Run! Use your wands!"

One of the newbies glanced at the others, confused. "What's a spindle?"

As he looked around, one of the ten-legged creatures leapt from the wall and landed on his chest. He screamed as the creature stared up with one robotic red eye before pushing its fangs into him, tossing him out of the game. Henry, having faced these creatures before, began flicking bolts of white light down the tunnel and the small orbs slammed against some of the spindles and turned them to dust.

"Get ready, boys. These things are fast, and they're about to be on top of us," Henry yelled.

One of the boys threw a fireball, smashing three of them. "Use your orbs! Turn them to dust!"

Henry used his magic to help him run up the side of the wall, then somersaulted and landed on top of two of the largest creatures. He slashed his wand back and forth, hitting the creatures with the shots of magic and watched them disintegrate. His teammates seemed to be on top of things. Orbs of fire flew around the place, and only one of their teammates had been sent back so far.

Henry backed up toward his team, forming a line with them, and held his wand out in front of him like the others. "On the count of three, send one long stream that covers the entire tunnel. One, two, three!"

The team's combined stream of magic swirled through the entire tunnel, knocking the creatures to the ground and turning them to dust. When the light had receded and no more red eyes could be seen, Henry bent over and put his hands on his knees, laughing. "Well, hell. I wonder if the others are having such a hard time…"

Wyatt took his team to one of the older neighborhoods, scanning the three-story brick brownstones along the way. When he reached the last one on the block, he saw the shimmer of a treasure chest on the top floor. It wasn't the final trophy, but it was a clue to where they could find it, so it was important that he got there first.

Wyatt pointed up at the window and put his finger in front of his lips. "If there is a clue box, then there's danger close by. Keep your ears and eyes open."

They all nodded and slowly followed Wyatt across the crumbling Chicago street and through the open door of the brownstone. As they stepped through, some sort of winged creature flew overhead squawking loudly. Everyone turned their magic toward it, but it was just a bird. The real danger pounced from the other room—a street gang, an old-school Chicago street gang, armed with guns, knives, and even wands.

Wyatt pushed the guys back as they got ready to fight.

"Use your skills, boys. This is where it counts. We gotta get to that chest."

The guys exchanged magical blows with the street gang, dodged bullets, and tried not to get hit by flying knives. Some of the street gang resorted to full-out hand-to-hand combat, which the guys were excited about since they'd been working out for the last three weeks. One of the younger guys got caught in the corner by a gun-toting gang member.

The kid put his hand in the air with a ball of light in his palm. "You silly guy, you never bring a gun to an elf fight."

The fireball slammed into the guy's face, knocking him across the room and into the wall. As soon as he hit the wall, he disintegrated into thin air. That was something most of the dangers did when they defeated a character in the virtual world. Wyatt looked at the kid and nodded, giving him props.

As the team kept fighting, Wyatt quietly snuck around the combatants and vaulted the railing of the staircase. He nodded at his team to let them know he would be back as soon as he could and needed them to cover for him. He crept slowly to the third floor where the chest holding the hint sat, glimmering gold.

"Not so fast. That's mine," a voice said from the right.

Wyatt turned quickly and jumped backward. A gang member stood in the corner, tattoos covering his arms, his neck, and even part of his face. Wyatt grabbed the hint from the box and looked at the gang member, who was now standing in front of his exit. He glanced down at the desk and snatched a letter opener, holding it stiffly as he took a deep breath.

"This is going to be the play of the century," Wyatt muttered as he took off across the room toward the guy.

When he got closer, the guy pulled a knife. Wyatt dropped to his knees, slid across the wooden floor, and stabbed the letter opener into his gut as he passed between his legs and out into the hallway. He didn't stop to look back, just started running. When he reached the bottom level, the team was waiting for him. They'd defeated the other gang members.

He held the hint up in the air and smiled. "I got it!"

All the guys looked at him and didn't say a word, just stared. His brows came together, and he looked at everyone, unsure what was going on. "Didn't you hear me? I got the hint!"

He followed their eyes to his chest and saw a knife embedded in it. He sighed and shook his head, knowing what was coming. As he began to flicker, he tossed the hint to one of his teammates and closed his eyes, reappearing out on the field with the others who had been tossed from the game.

He slammed his hands against his legs. "Dammit!"

***

"All right, we know the treasure's in there," Luke said, pointing to the glass balcony of the Willis Tower.

One of the others blinked his eyes and looked at Luke. "Yeah. Dangers will be in there too, wanting to fight us in a glass room hundreds of stories in the air."

Luke chuckled and slapped him on the shoulder. "Don't

you love this game? The best way is just go in full-force and face whatever is waiting for us."

The guys grabbed their wands and readied their magic. The glass balcony was a small space, but that didn't mean there wouldn't be all kinds of hell loose in there. Luke stood up and took a deep breath, facing the doorway into the viewing area. He nodded, and they slowly walked toward the door, ready for anything.

Out in the stands, both strangers and friends dressed in Cardinals colors stood with bated breath as both teams played back and forth. The Cardinals players couldn't see the other team and vice versa, but the spectators could see everything, and they knew both teams were really close to the win.

Izzie bit the inside of her cheek and held tightly to the rail in front of her as the team headed for the balcony. "Come on, you can do this. Just a little bit more."

Inside the game, Luke stepped out of the doorway into the area where the treasure was. The glass panels were intact, but that didn't mean they were safe, He knew that they needed to avoid the glass floor as much as possible. Before he could say anything to his team, the building shook slightly, and loud squeaks filled their ears. The sound dropped them to their knees, and they covered their ears with their hands.

One of the guys looked at Luke. "What the hell was that? It sounded like a horde of giant rats!"

Just as the kid said it, Luke looked up and saw dozens of three-foot-tall rats closing on the group. "Well, they said Chicago had rats, but I didn't know they were like these sonsofbitches."

Without any prompting, the team jumped to their feet and sent long streams of fire toward the rats. They could hear the squealing and gnashing of teeth as the magic swirled around the horde, pushing the rats back. They were a threat, but Luke could tell they weren't the ultimate threat.

One of the guys ran to the side and flicked his wand toward one of the windows at the back, shattering it and opening the room to the outside. "Push them through the hole!"

The guys used their magic to push them until the last of the rats fell screeching to its furry, splattered death, then turned to Luke, excited. A second later, their eyes moved past him to whatever was standing behind him. Slowly, he turned around and clenched his fists. A large werewolf stood in front of him, breathing heavily and snarling.

Luke dropped his weapon and took off his vest, letting it fall to the floor. He looked back at the guys and nodded. "I got this one."

Out in the stands, the crowds cheered wildly as they watched Luke shift halfway into his wolf form—his claws long, his eyes yellow, and his teeth sharp. The two wolves charged and traded blows, swipes, and bites. All that could be heard were whimpering and yelps. Izzie held tightly to the rail, shaking it every time Luke took a blow. The other wolf picked Luke up and threw him across the room, slamming him into one of the panes of glass, which cracked.

Luke took a deep breath, then looked at the wolf with glowing yellow eyes and growled, not willing to be taken out by a virtual werewolf when he was the real thing.

He wrinkled his nose and dug his claws into the floor. "You've come for the wrong wolf."

Luke lunged forward, leapt into the air, grabbed the wolf by the shoulders as he flew over him, and flung the wolf into a window. They both hit the glass and Luke dug his claws into the floor, watching as the pane shattered. The werewolf couldn't hold on and fell out the window, yelping and howling all the way to the ground.

Luke rose on one knee, keeping his head down as he transformed back into his human form, then stood up and looked at his teammates.

They were silent for several moments, but when the treasure appeared beside Luke, they began to clap and cheer. He was the hero of that game. Luke reached down and grabbed the trophy, sending all the players back to the field. As soon as he opened his eyes, he saw the entire stadium on their feet cheering wildly for their victorious Cardinals. They were one step closer to regionals, and Luke was one step closer to being accepted.

17

All the leaves had fallen to the ground, creating a lot of work for Horace, but it announced to the students that November was there. Halloween had come and gone. The group was over it before the holiday had arrived, since just a couple of days before they had released a horde of spirits on the campus, then managed to get them back to the World in Between. To them, November was welcome, and everyone was excited that the holidays were getting close.

Professor Ira Heineken stood at the front of the garage, holding his wand in front of him. "Welcome, everyone, to this year's mechanics and magics class. My name is Professor Ira Heineken. I just transferred from San Francisco."

Professor Heineken was tall, with shoulder-length blond hair that he pulled back into a man-bun at the nape of his neck. His eyes were crystal blue, and his smile was perfect and white. He looked exactly like the kind of professor who would come from California.

The professor took a deep breath and looked at each student, knowing that not all of them would be happy about this class. "This class is about essentials. Everyone needs to know how to work on cars, or any motorized vehicle you might own. I'm going to show you how anybody can fix a car using their magic, and not even get a speck of dirt on their clothes most of the time."

Kathleen scoffed and rolled her eyes. "Right. I've seen my father try to work on a car. It looks like he just came back from mining coal by the time he's done. Don't we have car people to do this for us?"

The professor overheard what Kathleen said and pointed at her. "You're right! There are people to do this for you, but everyone should know how to change a tire, check their oil, and change their oil. Besides, with the busy lives you will have when you get out of school, wouldn't you like to be able to do car maintenance in five minutes instead of sitting at a dirty and dusty mechanic's shop waiting for the humans to take forty minutes or three hours to do the same thing? I promise you, Kathleen, by the end of this class you'll be able to change your own oil, and you'll be able to change your tire without having to touch it."

Kathleen lifted an eyebrow. "I'll take that challenge, but I'm not the kind of girl who changes tires."

Everyone laughed and nodded. No one could imagine Kathleen doing anything with a car. Still, she might be giving him a hard time but wasn't completely uninterested in the subject. Besides, they were all of driving age and were dying to get behind the wheel of the car. This would give them another skill and get them one step closer to it.

Ethan raised his hand, and the professor nodded at him. "My father was a mechanic, from what I've been told. My uncle owns a mechanic shop too, so I've learned a lot over the years about working on cars."

The professor looked impressed. "Did you use magic?"

Ethan shrugged. "My uncle's not magical, but I did use magic on some things. I guess I learned the human and the magical way at the same time."

The professor smiled. "Then you'll really appreciate learning how to do it all the magical way."

Peter rubbed his hands together, looking at Ethan and smiling. "This is freaking awesome."

The professor pulled a tarp off what looked to be a car and held out his arms. "Here you go! This is what we're going to fix up in this class. Can anyone tell me what it is?"

Kathleen leaned toward Emma and whispered, "The leftovers from the recycling facility?"

Peter put his hand up excitedly. "It's a 1976 Chevette hatchback! And it looks like it was a pale metallic blue, which is pretty awesome because that only came from the factory."

The professor pointed at Peter. "Exactly right! Now that I have your interest, I'm going to drop a bomb on you. I lied. Not everything in life can be fixed with magic, so I'm going to show you how to fix these things manually, then tell you what spells you can use to enhance as you go along."

Kathleen threw her hands in the air. "I knew it."

The professor chuckled. "Don't worry, Kathleen. We'll still get you there. Now, gather around. We're gonna start by pulling off all the things that need to be either replaced or fixed and then put back on. I want you to point out different pieces and tell me why you think they should go."

Kathleen and Emma walked to the back of the car and looked down at the bumper, which was barely hanging on. "I think this silver piece back here might need to be…fixed?"

The professor walked to the back of the car, trying to figure out what they were talking about. "Oh, you mean the fender?"

Emma and Kathleen just stared at him.

He chuckled. "Yes, we will fix this fender and reuse it if we possibly can. The problem with some of these things is that they are rusted, and some of them are rusted beyond fixing. When that's the case, we will order the part and learn how to put it on fresh and new."

Peter popped up from under the hood. He'd given everything a thorough inspection. "There's a lot in here you can't use, and there's a lot that they don't make any more. We can either buy secondhand, or we're going to have to adjust to fit the new technologies."

The professor nodded. "Aha! This is where magic can come in handy. We can take any part, use some magic, and custom-fit it to this car to make it work. You might not be able to explain it very well to the humans, but at least we won't be changing the functionality of the car. Very good, Peter. Anyone else?"

All the guys were ecstatic, and even some of the girls, like Aya, but it was definitely a class Kathleen wasn't going to enjoy.

18

"All right, class, today we are going to do something that I think you're really going to enjoy," Professor Eleanor Hudson said as she walked to the front of the class, situating her black-rimmed glasses on her nose.

The group was sitting close together, happy that they were going to be doing something interactive. Their junior year history class hadn't been very exciting up to that point, and they were quickly losing interest. Especially Ethan, since he wasn't one to read the textbook.

Professor Hudson pulled out a glass bowl and set it on the table in front of her. "I want each student to come up—please be orderly—and pull a name out of the bowl, then return to your seat."

The students got in line and made their way toward the front. Each student pulled out a piece of paper and looked down at the name. Some they recognized, and others they had never heard of. When the entire class had picked a name and returned to their seats, the professor set the bowl to the side, smiling at the students.

"Okay, this is what we're going to do today. I know that reading from a textbook and lectures can be really boring, so I figured a much more interactive approach to history might get your attention. Today, we are going to play a game. This will be much like Louper, only you won't have to defeat any enemies or reach any treasures."

Everyone in the class started to whisper to each other, excited about the idea. Izzie looked at Luke and winked, making his cheeks turn red.

Professor Hudson put up her hand to quiet the class. "On each of the pieces of paper is a name, which is who you will become when I put the spell over the class. You will be able to walk through your surroundings and learn about that character's time period in history, all while seated at your desks. Does anyone have any questions?"

Ethan slowly put his hand up. "Does it matter if I'm a woman?"

Everyone laughed, and Kathleen looked at Ethan with raised eyebrows. "I think it'll be good for you."

The professor chuckled and shook her head. "No, Ethan, it doesn't matter if you're a woman in this magical world. I promise you will be a man when you come back."

Ethan grumbled, "Better be."

Kathleen smirked and looked at Emma. "Personally, I would love to see Ethan in a dress. I think he would be a beautiful woman."

Ethan stuck his tongue out at her and looked back at the professor, waiting for the event to start. The professor flicked her wand down each row of the students. Blue and purple light flashed, swirling around each seat and up and through each person, settling them in their chairs.

Kathleen found herself standing in the Light Elf palace. She looked around the room, then down at herself, realizing quickly that she was the Light Elf Queen. She giggled and walked over to a mirror. Staring back at her was the fair skin and beautiful complexion of the current queen on Oriceran. "I could definitely get used to this."

"I think I could too," a voice said from the left.

Kathleen turned and saw the Light Elf king walking clumsily toward her. She realized that it was another student, but because the voice was the king's, she didn't recognize the person. He put his hand out and bowed. "It's Emma."

Kathleen laughed loudly. "We ended up in the same place. How awesome is that?"

For Izzie and Alison, things were a lot more exciting. When they opened their eyes, they weren't on the same world, but they were both facing the same situation. They were prophets, those who could foresee the future, like the ones who had foreseen the beginning of the Golden Age and the end of Oriceran decades before.

Izzie looked around. She was in a small cabin, and when she walked to the window, she saw that she was in a kemana, but stuck far at the back with guards at the front.

For Alison, it was different. She could see the souls and energy around her, but she was in the middle of a prophecy. The words she spoke came fluidly, like she was in a dream watching but watching very closely. She was discussing the end of Oriceran, and it made her sad.

The other students were different creatures. Some were leaders of the dragons, while others were brave warriors. Ethan found himself in the very uncomfortable shoes of one of the first witches who crossed from Oriceran to Earth. Unfortunately, she had come at a time when witches weren't very welcome. Ethan spent the entire time being chased and using his magic—or her magic—to try to get away.

Luke was probably the one the most comfortable, and not just because he played Louper. He found himself in a shifter body, but not just any shifter. He was the leader of the shifters from two decades before, when he had created a sanctuary for the others. He witnessed the horrible things the dark families did to the shifters, and by the time the class was over, he could feel anger and resentment in his heart.

It was safe to say from the silence that reigned when the spell dissipated that this class had affected them strongly.

19

"Okay, Izzie and Peter, you two are going to go into the restricted section, so play it cool until you get the signal from us," Ethan whispered as Librarian Decker casually put books away on the shelf behind them.

Izzie and Peter nodded and looked down at the books on the desk in front of them, pretending to read them. They needed to get into the restricted section, but it was against the rules for any student to go into the cage without express permission from the headmistress.

Ethan blinked at Kathleen and she walked over to the librarian, tapping him on the shoulder. "Excuse me, Librarian Decker, I was wondering if you could help me find a book. I'm really interested in potions, and I was wondering if there was a potion that would help me increase the size of my… wardrobe in my room."

The librarian let out a sigh of relief and nodded, stepping down off the stool. "Of course. There's a whole section back in the right-hand corner about potions making."

Kathleen smiled and glanced at Ethan as she followed the small librarian down the rows of books. All along the shelves was sparkling lettering and even some labels that produced bubbles as he passed by them.

The librarian walked about three-quarters of the way down the aisle and stopped, then pulled over a ladder and climbed up to the right shelves. "This book should have everything you need about home renovations using potions. Though, I can't help but wonder why you wouldn't just use your wand. Potions can be such a mess. If even the slightest thing is off, you could end up with a willow tree in your closet instead of an extension."

Kathleen feigned surprise. "I didn't even think about that! Could you show me where those books are?"

Emma came around the corner. "There you are, Librarian Decker. I was hoping you could show me the section on mystics. I really wanted to brush up on my fortune-telling for next year."

The librarian lifted an eyebrow and waved his arm in the air. "Sure. It's on the way to where Kathleen needs to go anyway."

The librarian looked at them suspiciously as he led them to the sections they'd requested. He led Emma down the rarely-used section of books on mystics and fortune-telling and pointed out different books for her to look at. "These are all something you will learn in your senior year. Try mystics for beginners, so you don't become a prophet out of nowhere."

Emma nodded and smiled at Kathleen as the librarian quickly took off down the aisle. Kathleen followed him, glancing at the cage as Izzie and Peter snuck inside and closed the door behind them. The librarian looked at Kathleen, and she leaned against the bookcase to shield them from his view. "Oh, I should've known exactly where these were."

The librarian grumbled and started to leave. Panicked not to let him go anywhere near the restricted section, Kathleen knocked several books off the shelf, grabbing his attention. "Dang, I'm so sorry."

Librarian Decker waved her away. "Just go find what you need. I'll take care of this. There's always something going on in this library. I can never get any work done."

In the restricted section, Izzie looked up and down the rows of books, unsure exactly what she'd be able to find. "Many of these books are in another language. How am I supposed to find anything?"

Peter shrugged. "I don't know, but we gotta try. We need a spell that might work against the dark wizards—if we can find them."

Izzie sighed and pulled a book down from the shelf. "You're right. We need something simple but effective. With all these books, there has to be something here."

Peter closed one of the books and put it back on the shelf. "You're right, there has to be something here. Otherwise, we might be in big trouble. The whole *school* might be in big trouble."

"Look," said Izzie, "there's nothing in these. We're going to have to try again later."

Librarian Decker finished putting the books back up on the shelf and looked at the main area of the library. He didn't see Peter or Izzie as he walked over to the phone on the desk. He was going to bring in another gnome to help keep an eye on the students. They seemed to always get themselves in trouble, especially when he couldn't watch them closely enough.

"What do you mean, you need help keeping track of the students?" the gnome on the phone asked.

Librarian Decker got angry. "Why do you question me? There are a ton of students in here today, and everyone is asking for help with something strange. Stuff that's out of the ordinary, given what they usually look for. I just have this feeling that something's going on. I need to keep track of these kids before they get themselves and the school in trouble."

The gnome on the other end said, "I'll be right down. Have you kept track of the restricted section?"

Librarian Decker glanced at it, but the door was shut, so he didn't think much about it. "Of course, I have! These students know not to go in there, and they'd be pretty brazen to do so right in the middle of the day while I'm standing in the library! Just get down here and make it snappy. If one of the students tried to get in behind my back, there would be hell to pay."

Emma stood in the parking lot rubbing her shoulder and watching as Ethan maneuvered the car quickly through the cones and around the corner to a perfect stop. "For somebody who was so nervous about this, he sure has gotten comfortable behind the wheel."

Kathleen glanced at her and smirked. "You sound angry

about that. Don't worry, Emma, he fixed the fence really fast, and your shoulder will be fine."

Emma huffed. "Not worried about my shoulder or the fence. I'm worried about the fact that I just completely bombed practice for the day. Who knew that the rabbit was going to jump out of nowhere?"

Kathleen giggled and put her arm around her friend. "True, but you probably should've pressed the brake instead of the gas. It was actually quite funny. I don't think I've ever seen a professor's eyes grow so big so fast. Everyone thought for certain that you were just going to keep going and plow through the woods."

Emma kept a straight face. "It's not funny."

Luke elbowed her and glanced at Izzie with a smile. "It's *kinda* funny. I think you'll see that once you're no longer upset about taking down the fence."

Emma gave him a blank stare. "Oh, sure, that's easy for you to say. You were terrible the first day, and all of a sudden you've got it down pat."

Izzie laughed and rubbed Luke's shoulder. "I don't think taking down two of the three cones is 'having it down pat.'"

Emma shrugged. "Yeah, at least it was the cones and not the fence."

Luke pouted and looked at Izzie. "I'm sorry. We can't all be master drivers like you. Who taught you to drive like that, anyway? You swerved in and out of those cones like you were a racecar driver, then made a perfect stop—all without breaking a sweat."

Alison tapped Luke on the shoulder and pointed to her

forehead. "She might not be sweating, but I can tell you that *I* was slightly panicked."

Izzie pointed at Alison. "See? She couldn't even see where I was going, no offense, Alison, and she was panicked. That doesn't make me a good driver. There's more to driving than not knocking things down."

Kathleen smiled. "It's okay, Izzie. You're allowed to be proud of being a good driver. Don't let these grumps take that away from you."

Luke put his arm around Izzie and gave the others a defiant stare. "I just want to point out that I'm very proud of Izzie for being such an excellent driver. On top of that, if I happen to fail my driving test and this class, my girlfriend will drive me wherever I need to go."

Izzie laughed and smacked him in the chest. "Is that all you're keeping me around for?"

Luke chuckled. "Hey, it's a good attribute to have."

20

Professor Max Regency stood at the door of the classroom as the students filed in. As Luke and some of the other Louper players entered, he gave them high fives. "Great job on the game, guys. Very good job. I have a good feeling about the first tournament."

The Louper players laughed and gave him high fives while the other students rolled their eyes, obviously over that last win and ready for the next. When all the students were seated, Professor Regency made his way to the front of the class and rubbed his hands together.

The professor was excited about this class. It covered one of the subjects he loved the most—the veil between the living and the dead. "Everyone take a seat and quiet down. We have a lot to do today."

Several students groaned, but Professor Regency didn't seem to notice. When the students had quieted, he waved his hands and dimmed the lights, making it almost eerie in the classroom. He chuckled when some of the students looked around, creeped out by the pictures he had on the walls.

He began his lecture in a spooky voice and kept the interested smile on his face. "Today, we are going to dive into the world where the living cannot go. There are certain places in both our worlds—Earth or Oriceran—where the veil between the living and the dead is thin and allows us to communicate with those in the World in Between."

Professor Regency walked up and down the aisles, touching those who were half-asleep on the shoulder and startling them awake. "One day of the year, Halloween, the energy is just right, and it becomes possible for anyone with even the slightest bit of magic to communicate with the dead."

Izzie, Kathleen, and the others glanced in Alison's direction and saw the nervous look that crossed her face. They had all met some of the dead from the World in Between, and they were the ones who had sent them back there. Izzie shifted in her seat uncomfortably and clenched her hands on the desk.

Oh God, this just might be where we're found out. Will they show up and give us away, or can they tell everyone about who helped them get out? What if they could tell us who the dark forces were?

A flurry of questions went through Izzie's mind, but there wasn't much she could do about it at that point. Professor Regency cleared his throat, grabbing her attention as he passed her desk. "Sometimes, when the veil isn't thin all over, parts of it can be enhanced with spells. I've found a spot near the window in this very room that has sometimes proven lucky for having a figure appear from the World in Between and give us a quick wave. Would you like to see?"

The interest was mixed within the classroom. Some of the people nodded their heads excitedly while others shook theirs and covered their faces with their hands. He laughed loudly and shot out a ball of light that hovered by the window.

"*Erectus deceased. Show us where the veil is incomplete,*" he chanted.

The ball of light shimmered and shook, and sparks dropped to the floor. As the students watched, an image of a woman began to appear. A hush fell over the classroom when the students saw her and waited with bated breath to see what would happen.

The woman, older in years with long silvery hair, looked more than worried as she scanned the class, and her eyes stopped on Izzie. She pointed straight at her, jabbing her finger in Izzie's direction over and over as if in warning. Everyone in the classroom gasped and looked between the woman and Izzie, who couldn't keep her eyes off the ghost. Fear slammed into her chest.

Just as the woman opened her mouth to speak, the spell faded, and the woman was pulled back to the World in Between. The students' voices rose excitedly as they looked at Izzie.

"Why was she pointing at Izzie?" one of the students asked.

"I don't know, but it seems kind of suspicious to me, especially since we thought she might be a toombie," another one whispered.

Professor Regency quieted the class. "Everyone! Pay attention! There's no reason to be talking amongst yourselves. I have to wonder, though, what exactly that was about. Do you have any idea, Izzie?"

Izzie and the rest of the group sat there trying to look as innocent and clueless as possible. "I have no idea, Professor."

The professor shrugged and let out a sigh figuring it might've just been a bad spell. Izzie leaned toward Alison and whispered, "What in the world?"

Alison shook her head. "I have no idea, but I don't think it has anything to do with me letting them free. I don't know. We can talk about it after class."

Professor Regency didn't wait for the rest of the students to file out of the class when the bell rang. Instead, he gathered his things and left ahead of them. He glanced at several of the older students in the hallway who were staring. They'd noticed the slight bit of panic on the professor's face. The professor ignored them and marched out into the entryway, where students were gathering for lunch.

"Watch out, coming through!" Professor Regency was in a hurry, but the students didn't seem to want to get out the way.

He finally was able to push his way through the crowd and into the hallway where the administration offices were located. He smoothed down his vest and rolled the sleeves of his shirt up to his elbows before continuing. The last thing he wanted to do was look completely taken back by what happened, but it had been pretty strange. He knocked on the door of the headmistress's office and waited.

"Come in," she called.

Professor Regency turned the doorknob and walked into the room. He took the time to close the door behind him, not wanting anyone else to hear what he was about to say.

The headmistress looked up in surprise as the professor climbed into one of her chairs. "Professor Regency, what is it? You look like you saw a ghost."

Professor Regency chuckled, then presented the headmistress with a straight face. "I'll be honest with you. I just did a spell to speak to a ghost in the World in Between, Instead of the sunshiny ghost we usually get, I got an older woman who stared right at Izzie and pointed at her like it was a warning. You had told me that you wanted to know if anything strange happened with Izzie, and I think this qualifies."

Headmistress Berens tried to maintain a neutral expression since she didn't want everyone to know she was that worried about Izzie. "Thank you for letting me know, Professor. It definitely sounds strange, and I'll do some research into it. Please continue to keep an eye out for things like that. We never know when it could be something very important."

The professor hopped down from the chair and nodded, turning toward the door. "Absolutely, Headmistress. Let me know if you need my help."

Headmistress Berens waited until the professor left the room before hurrying to the door. She gathered her composure and walked out, locking the door behind her and made her way toward the entryway. There were so many students standing around the entryway that it irritated her. She pressed her wand to her throat so she'd be heard over the din. "If you don't want to go to the cafeteria you don't have to, but you can't stand here, so keep it moving!"

The students immediately moved aside as the headmistress made her way down the hall and around the corner to the library. When she entered, she was glad to see that it was empty except for the librarian, Leo Decker.

Decker looked up at the headmistress in surprise. He knew that something was troubling her by the look on her face. "Has something else happened?"

Professor Berens looked over her shoulder and locked the door with her magic. "During channeling class with Professor Regency, they thinned the veil like they do every year, but this time a ghost stood pointing at Izzie like it was a warning."

Librarian Decker looked at her for a moment and rubbed his chin. "You do remember that the living and the dead in the World in Between can observe everything. They can be anywhere at any time. They must know the danger is close. I hate to say this, but given that and everything else that's happened, something terrible might be coming."

The headmistress nodded and walked over to the window, looking out across the fields. "I've had that feeling, and this doesn't surprise me. Do you think that the wards around the school are enough? I mean, should we add more?"

Librarian Decker nodded. "Do we have any idea what they are *not* using right now?"

The headmistress turned toward him and leaned against the window sill. "I don't know. I was told what type of spell it is, but I wasn't told where they are or what the other options were at the time. It all seemed straightfor-ward to me."

Librarian Decker jumped down from his ladder and stood in front of her. "It's okay. I can investigate this and get back to you. I would have to say that the woods are probably the most vulnerable."

The headmistress turned back and looked at the perimeter of the grounds. "You're right. That fence doesn't go through the woods. Only the wards are able to go through there. We have to keep this school and everyone in it safe."

21

Izzie stabbed her fork into her chicken nugget, dipped it in the ketchup, took a bite of it, and put the fork back down. She'd lost her appetite after what had happened earlier. Everything was getting stranger by the second, and she needed something to do to keep her mind off it.

Kathleen sighed and pushed the food around on her plate. "Anyone have any ideas to keep us busy this afternoon? Apparently, there's something going on in the kemana and the students aren't allowed down there, so that's out of the question."

Peter shrugged looking just as bored. "I have no idea. I'm tired of walking the grounds. I got kicked out of most of the shifty bars I went to after they figured out I was just glamoured, and there's nothing going on with the school paper."

Ethan grinned mischievously. "I have an idea. I want you all to meet me out by the garage."

Aya lifted an eyebrow and looked at him. "What are you up to?"

Ethan chuckled. "It's a surprise. Just meet me out there."

Emma nodded. "I'll do it. Why not? Nothing else going on."

"I'm in," Peter chimed in.

Kathleen looked at Izzie and shrugged. "Why not? I might as well do something exciting with my time off."

Aya let her plate fade away and grabbed her bookbag. "Sorry, guys. I got too much homework. I gotta get caught up."

Alison followed her. "Yeah, sorry. I gotta finish my homework too. I've been too invested in what we were looking for and got behind."

Ethan looked at Jennifer and wiggled his eyebrows. "How about you?"

Jennifer chuckled and shook her head. "No, thanks. I have homework, and I don't really feel like getting in trouble today."

Ethan watched the others walk out of the cafeteria and cringed as Jason walked up to the table. He patted Ethan hard on the back and looked around as Alison disappeared. "I heard you guys talking. I'm down. Besides, I was trying to stay close to Alison, but she obviously has homework to do."

Kathleen scoffed. "You know that's called stalking, right? And besides, she has a boyfriend."

Jason put his hands up. "Hey, I'm just looking out for her best interests." He gave a wide smile and shrugged as he walked off, doing his best to look uninterested.

Ethan rolled his eyes and shrugged, standing up and waving to the others to follow him. "This'll be easier without him. Let him go. We gotta be quiet if we do this, but I promise it will be worth it."

The group walked out of the mansion and followed Ethan toward the garage where they had been working on the car. As they approached, Ethan put his hand up. "Wait here."

Ethan snuck around the back of the garage, and they heard him crunching in the leaves and grunting loudly. The group looked at each other for a second and peeked around the corner as Ethan pushed the Chevette they had been working on out into the open.

He held out his hand and smiled. "I figured we could drive into town. Come on, let's go."

Izzie crossed her arms over her chest. "I don't know about this. We could get in one heap of trouble by doing this."

Luke shrugged and nudged her, smiling slyly. "Come on, let's just do it. It'll make for one hell of a story when we're older."

Emma look like she wanted to protest, but when Izzie grinned and climbed into the backseat with Luke she relaxed, figuring why the heck not? Emma got in the back with Izzie and Luke. Kathleen and Peter walked up to the front passenger door and looked at each other.

Kathleen looked over the hood at Ethan and bit her bottom lip. "I don't know. I mean, I'm all about an adventure, but this goes a little bit too far."

Peter shrugged and flung open the door, climbing into the center of the front seat. "Hey, I'm all about doing adventurous things now, I guess. Come on, Kathleen, it'll be fun."

Kathleen looked at Peter in shock, then shrugged and got in. "There must be something in the water if Peter is willing to do something this crazy. I hope you know what you're doing, Ethan."

Ethan laughed and climbed into the driver's seat. "Just relax. I got this."

Ethan started the car and drove toward the gate. They quickly pushed it open and sped through, not wanting to get caught right there at the entrance. Ethan decided that taking back roads was probably the best option so that they wouldn't pass any of the professors on the way out.

Ethan hung his hand out the window as he drove down the winding road. "See? Easy-peasy."

Just then there was a jolt, and Ethan pumped the brakes but nothing happened. Kathleen's head snapped to the side, and she looked at him wide-eyed. "What's going on?"

Ethan shook his head in panic, not knowing what to do. "The brakes went out."

Peter put Ethan's hand back on the steering wheel and nodded at him with wide eyes. "Calm down. We learned how to do this in Mechanics and Magics Class. We can figure out how to stop this."

Ethan took a deep breath. "You're right. You and I can use our magic to work on the brakes while I steer the car."

Izzie leaned forward and put her hand on Kathleen's shoulder. "Me and you, we'll use our magic to keep the car steady while it goes around the corners."

Kathleen nodded. "Got it."

Luke flung open the passenger door. "I'll use my strength to slow the car down. If you lose me, don't forget to come back and get me."

Izzie looked at him like he was crazy. "Are you sure?"

Luke scoffed. "Yeah, I got this. Just keep the car nice and steady."

Luke jumped out of the car and rolled across the gravel as Izzie looked out the back window, watching him. He jumped to his feet and raced after the car. He ran faster than any human Izzie had ever seen before, but then, Luke wasn't human—not entirely. He caught up to the car and grabbed the bumper, digging his heels in as the car dragged him.

Peter had his eyes closed as Ethan helped him work on the brakes while swerving back and forth on the winding roads. "I just about got it. Keep it steady."

It took some serious muscle, both magical and brute strength, but after about ten minutes of swerving, the car slowed down and eventually came to a stop. Luke leaned over the trunk and breathed heavily, and the others sat quietly in their seats, shocked by what had just happened.

Peter shook his head. "I only fixed it enough to stop. We can't do that again. We're going to have to push this car back to school."

Kathleen crossed her arms and looked angrily at Ethan. "Oh, you have this, do you?"

Ethan smiled uncomfortably and shrugged. "I guess maybe I should've waited until after we finished."

Kathleen raised an eyebrow. "You think?"

They piled out of the car and stood in front of it, staring at the long winding road then back toward the school. Kathleen sighed and pulled out her wand using just a little magic to enhance the night sky and light their way. Izzie turned toward the woods and sent out a small orb of light, asking the faeries for help. As the group pushed, small little faeries danced around them then gathered at the front of the car to help turn the car around and push.

Ethan looked down surprised as the speed picked up. "Strong little buggers."

Luke smiled and tapped the trunk in a familiar rhythm. "We might as well sing while we push. It'll help the time pass."

Izzie smiled. "Good idea. What song are you thinking about?"

Luke and Ethan looked at each other and smiled. "None other than the school fight song, of course."

They all began to sing, even Kathleen, who was more than bitter about having to push a car back to the school.

"We fight with all our might. We are the Cardinals!" Everyone cheered out the last line, as they pushed and laughed. They figured that there was no reason to be angry about the situation.

Kathleen elbowed Ethan and gave him a smile. "Would've been a good plan if it hadn't failed so miserably."

Ethan laughed. "You know me, always pushing the boundaries."

Peter wiped his forehead and put his hands back on the trunk, trying to avoid the faeries. "At least we didn't go over the side of a cliff in a fiery ball of flames like we did in class."

Izzie giggled, and Emma smiled at Peter. "Yeah, thanks for that."

They pushed the car through the gate and back toward the garage. When they reached the doors, Ethan waved his wand and opened them up. The group gave one last push and left the car where it belonged. They walked back out, closing the doors behind them, and high-fived each other before turning to the faeries.

Izzie stepped forward to the closest fairy. "Thanks for helping us."

The fairy nodded and flew back to the others, and all of them waved their little hands as they flew off in different directions.

Peter looked at the mansion, then back at the others. "We better get back before we get caught."

Izzie put her arm around Ethan and smiled as the group started for the mansion. "Well, we never made it to town, but I can't say we didn't still have an adventurous night."

The air was getting cold, but that didn't stop the students from gathering outside. They were dressed in their uniforms, and excited for the alumni welcome that was about to take place. It was a special time of year, a time when all the SNM alumni from all the different years returned to the school to participate in all kinds of activities with the current students.

Some had attended when the school had first opened, and some just a few years before. Many of them wore the school's colors, while others stepped through portals from Oriceran in traditional costume. It was an exciting time for the students, something not everybody got to see.

"George," Professor Hudson said as she walked over to one of the older students climbing through a portal and hugged him.

"Professor Hudson, it's so good to see you," George replied.

Professor Hudson looked at his outfit. "I miss my days on Oriceran. How is everything over there?"

George gave her an update as they strolled. "Things are always changing…"

The headmistress moved around the courtyard welcoming the former students, hugging them, and laughing at some of the antics they had pulled.

"Do you remember the time all the sinks poured chocolate milk, and the bathtubs and showers ran with orange pudding?" one of the former students asked the headmistress.

The headmistress threw her head back and laughed loudly. "I *thought* that was you. You stayed the course, though. I admired your unwillingness to give in to me and my tactics."

The alumnus chuckled and shook his head. "You did make some serious threats, but my dad was a Silver Griffin, so I was used to being put on the spot like that."

She hugged him and looked at all the students standing at the courtyard's edges, watching the alumni flood in. "Well, I can promise you things haven't changed a lot since then. Some of their practical jokes feel like they came straight from your hands. What are you doing now?"

The student laughed. "I own a practical joke shop in a kemana near Las Vegas."

The headmistress nodded. "That does not surprise me in the least. At least you went with what you knew, which is more than I can say for a lot of the alumni here."

The whole event was absolutely amazing, and the students couldn't wait to talk to the alumni about their futures.

The Louper stadium's stands were full of students and alumni alike. They waved different flags and talked with their friends. This might not have been a serious match with the championship up for grabs, but a Louper match was just plain fun for the players and spectators alike. The Louper alumni faced off with the current team in a scenario of the headmistress' choosing.

Izzie stood in the stands and waved at Luke, who was smiling and excited about the match. The headmistress walked out onto the field and put her hand up, quieting the crowd. "Welcome everyone, alumni and students, to the alumni versus student Louper game!"

The whole crowd cheered loudly, waving their flags and whistling for their favorite players. The headmistress smiled and waited for the crowd to quiet again. "Everyone is waiting to hear what the scenario will be for this game. I've decided that this time they will play on the school grounds, still in a virtual world, but in a place that's familiar to both sides."

The crowd cheered again. They couldn't wait to see the old players. Some of them had gone on to play Louper professionally, and of course, the current team was nothing to scoff at.

Peter nudged Izzie and nodded at Ethan and Luke. "Look, they're giving the alumni the stink eye. It's hilarious. My dad told me they did this when he was in school. I'm stoked to see it."

Izzie nodded and looked at Luke worriedly. "Yeah, but I think both of them are underestimating the power of the older guys. Hopefully, they won't put too much of a hurting on Luke and Ethan."

Izzie and Peter looked at each other for a moment and burst into laughter, imagining Luke and Ethan getting taken down by older guys from a previous Louper team. "At least they can't see each other. All that can really happen is one team gets to the treasure before the other, right?"

Just then the headmistress put her hand up once again to quiet the crowd, and everyone stood there waiting excitedly. "Just one more thing. Since this isn't a typical Louper game and it's all for fun, I've made a little adjustment. For this game, both teams will be able to see each other inside the playing field, and they will be able to interact. I've already instructed both sides that there will be no hard feelings and no fights. This is a time for practical jokes and a whole lot of fun. I can't say that I have a favorite, so boys, just go out there and have some fun. Oh, and the treasure is pretty big for this one."

The current Louper team lined up and looked at each other, wanting to find the prize before the alumni. The alumni might be older, and some of them might have more experience than the team, but they had been playing and training for weeks.

Wyatt smacked Luke on the back and nodded. "You got this?"

Luke smiled and eyed the alumni. "Oh, yeah. We got these old guys."

Professor Powell walked to the center of the field and waited until the crowd quieted before pulling out his wand. "Good luck, and may the best side win."

He swirled the wand over his head and allowed the green lines of magic to shoot out, covering the entire field and both teams. The current players prepared themselves, closing their eyes and waiting for the spell to take hold. When they opened them, they were standing in the foyer of the mansion. The other team was not in sight.

Henry gathered them into a group and looked up to make sure no one was spying on them. "We know they're out here, but our goal is to get to the prize before they do. Remember, we can pull any kind of jokes we want to and cause any kind of stumbles that cause them to pull back. Have fun with this, but for God sakes, find the prize before they do or we'll never live it down."

The team put their hands together and shouted in their battle cry before breaking up into the three teams they'd used in the prior game. Luke took his team into the court-yard, where he felt more comfortable. "I've run these grounds a million times as my wolf. I know every inch of it. Let's start by making our way over to the barn, then we'll go through the forest. Keep your eyes open and have fun."

Luke and his team raced across the fields since there wasn't much cover. When they reached the barn, they pressed their backs against it and looked around to make sure no one was following them. They crept around the barn to the doors and carefully pushed them open, but there was no movement inside.

The team entered and looked for the treasure or a hint of where it might be. A loud crack sounded from above, and a flood of maple syrup rained down on them. They covered their faces and crouched, waiting for it to end. When the flow finally stopped, something else started.

Two alumni at the back of the barn cackled as they

stood next to two large fans. "You boys didn't use your brains, did you?"

Luke stepped forward to say something, but before he could, the older men flipped the fans on and blew feathers all over them. The crowd in the stands howled with laughter as Luke and the others walked out of the barn looking like chickens.

Luke plucked a feather from his forehead, and let it float to the ground. "Is someone going to use their wands to fix this, or are we just gonna walk around looking like giant freaking chickens?"

One of the guys jolted and pulled his sticky wand from his pocket. "I got this."

As the kid waved his wand, and the maple syrup and feathers disappeared, Luke looked back toward the mansion, wondering how the others were doing.

Henry and Wyatt met back up in the cafeteria after each group had searched the entire main floor of the mansion. In the library, they'd not only found several of the alumni, who threw grape-soda-filled balloons at them that chased them through the halls until finally breaking over their heads, but they'd also found a dozen Librarian Deckers on the hunt. It had been a brilliant move by the alumni, but Henry wasn't going down like that.

Henry, Wyatt, and the rest of the guys crouched behind the staircase, trying to control their laughter. "This is definitely going to get them, and it'll clear the way for us upstairs."

Ethan looked at the others. "I'm glad at least one of my tricks could be helpful."

Wyatt smiled, then shushed everybody as the alumni rounded the corner looking for them. "Here they come. Everybody down."

One of the leaders of the alumni walked through the foyer, looking back and forth but seeing no one. He chuckled. "I guess we can head upstairs. It looks like we scared the little guys away."

All the alumni chuckled as they made their way to the staircase, not paying attention to the wavering magic at the base of the stairs. As soon as they stepped forward, they fell directly through the floor and through a portal. When they landed, and the air cleared, they found themselves in a field on the other side of the grounds and chuckled.

The leader of the group wiped the grass off his hands and looked at the others. "I have to give it to the kids. That was a pretty good one."

Back inside the mansion, Wyatt, Henry, and the others cheered and gave each other high fives and patted Ethan on the back. Wyatt shook Ethan's hand. "That was some pretty good work there, buddy. I didn't get caught in your April Fools' prank last year, but I'm glad you created it."

Ethan smiled. "Thanks. I've got some really good stuff for this year too."

Henry slapped Wyatt on the back. "Well, what are we waiting for? Let's get upstairs. The treasure has to be there."

Wyatt motioned for Henry to go first. "Watch your step."

The boys hurried up the stairs and heard the hum of the

treasure coming from the boy's dorms. However, as they rounded the corner, they were lifted off their feet and cocooned inside some sort of webbing. Upside-down, Wyatt and Henry bounced next to each other. In front of them stood the other group of alumni, laughing.

The other leader reached for the treasure and shrugged. "Good try, boys. Maybe next year."

The alumni were tricky and had used their wits and magic to pull out a win, but Luke, as he appeared on the field realizing they had lost, made himself a promise that it wouldn't happen again.

23

Job Fair Day was one of the school year's most exciting for the juniors and seniors. They got to really see what was out there in the world, and what kind of magical positions they could take on so they wouldn't have to work strictly with humans. It was purposely held on the same weekend when the alumni were on the campus. After all, these weren't ordinary students going out into the marketplace.

These were magicals who were facing a future where magic would always play a part in a world that wasn't always sure what to do with them.

The school's alumni had mostly done well for themselves and were the best source for where to pursue their dreams.

The teachers had prepped them all year, giving them insights into the different jobs and letting them know which companies might be attending the job fair. Ethan wasn't excited. He was glad he had another year in high school, but the rest of them were stoked and waiting in line before the gym doors even opened.

Peter looked at Aya excitedly as the group walked inside. "I know where my first stop is going to be. I'm going right to the journalism for magical beings table. I've been waiting all year to talk to them."

Aya spotted the government area, which was the largest in the whole place. "I want to see what jobs the government has for magical beings. I know it's the government, but they have all sorts of things that you can do."

Everyone spread out, stopping at each table and listening to the representatives' presentations. On the stage, Headmistress Berens stood with her arms crossed beside General Anderson, who had finally retired but still insisted on coming to check on the school. He couldn't walk away until he knew everything was safe.

The general lifted an eyebrow and looked at the headmistress "I hear your magical ROTC program isn't going so well."

The headmistress grimaced. "I tried, general, but I think there's still distrust between the magical beings and the humans. Give it time. It's a new program. Eventually, people will start signing up."

The general smiled and nodded. "I know. I told them from the beginning it would be a longshot if we saw anything within the first five years. We had to try, though. This has turned out excellently, however. You've got the tech industry, the cooking industry, journalism, my people, and everything in between. I'm impressed."

The headmistress smiled mischievously and nodded

toward the back of the gym. "Oh, you haven't seen anything yet, general."

Just then a large portal opened with a crack, and sparks flew all over the place. The Oriceran Consulate had sent representatives to speak to the young magicals about their futures, possibly on their planet. The general was taken aback by the grandeur of all of it, but so were all the students who stood mesmerized by the people walking through in Oriceran finery.

The general cleared his throat uncomfortably. "Well, I didn't expect that. Then again, I didn't read the whole lineup, and it was probably in there."

The headmistress laughed. "It *was* in there, and in fact, the Consulate was in contact with your offices to set it all up. They figured it would be good to come and find people who wanted to work on helping to integrate our two worlds. No offense, but we definitely need some magical people leading the way for those coming from Oriceran."

The general nodded. "I won't fight you on that one. That is an absolute necessity. If the people of Earth are going to look out for themselves, then the people of Oriceran have to do so as well."

The headmistress looked at the general. "I was thinking more along the lines of, we should look out for each other."

A formal dinner was scheduled to let the students and the alumni mingle and get to know each other better. The ordinarily dull cafeteria was transformed with round tables covered in white linen tablecloths, beautiful China, white hydrangeas and floating candles lighting the entire room.

"Look at this," Kathleen exclaimed as they walked into the dining area.

Emma smiled. "I know, right? It looks amazing in here, like we're walking into a ballroom. I wish they would do this for our dances, although I have to say I do love when they glamour the floor the way they do."

Aya bounced up next to the two of them and looked down at the floor. "It *is* glamoured. They just made it like beautiful white marble instead of the normal magical color-changing things they usually do. They made the whole affair absolutely gorgeous."

The three of them walked up to Izzie and Luke, Izzie

kissed each of them on the cheek. "Speaking of gorgeous, look who just walked through the door."

They all turned, even Ethan, who was sitting in a chair fiddling with his thumbs, already bored. Walking through the doors were Alison and Tanner. Alison's dress was a beautiful sparkling red gown that cascaded over her slender hips to the floor. Her silver hair was pulled up in a perfect bun, and she had a pair of dangling earrings that hung down to her chin.

Peter walked up next to the others and whistled loudly. "Look at that beautiful lady."

Alison smiled and pointed to herself, then looked behind her jokingly. "Oh, this thing? I've had it hidden in my closet for the last three years."

Kathleen scoffed. "Yeah, right. I remember what you dressed like when you first got here."

Izzie wrinkled her nose. "It's not much different than the way she dresses now, and I like it."

Alison smiled toward Izzie's energy and nodded. "Thank you."

They all took a seat around one of the large tables and put their napkins in their laps. Appetizers appeared on each plate, and their glasses filled with sparkling apple cider.

Tanner picked his glass up and put on a snobbish look, making the others laugh. "Mmm. Yes, a nice 1956 apple cider. Delicious."

"How's everybody doing tonight?" Professor Powell asked as he walked up to the table with a smile.

Tanner choked a little as he swallowed his apple cider,

then grinned. "Well. We have all our friends here, and the place looks absolutely amazing."

One of the alumni walked up to Professor Powell and patted him on the shoulder, looking at the students. "It should. Professor Powell here did an amazing job. We pretty much left him on his own to decorate the place. The headmistress was a bit nervous, not that I blame her. We all remember what kind of goof you were when you were here."

Ethan wrinkled his forehead and looked at the professor. "You're an alumnus?"

The professor cleared his throat and looked extremely uncomfortable. "Yes. Nothing to make a big deal about, though."

The professor wasn't happy at all that the alumnus had brought up the fact that he was once a student there. He had a lot of bad memories associated with that time in his life. He almost hadn't taken the job at the school because of it, but the problem really wasn't the school, it was the events that had taken place during that period.

Professor Powell looked at the students and smiled awkwardly. "Well, you guys have a good night. I've got other people to talk to. And keep the pranks to a minimum, Ethan. And by minimum, I mean zero."

Ethan shrugged as the professor walked away, then leaned in and whispered to the group, "It's so strange that he's an alumnus, yet he never tells anyone. I feel like the alumni here are shouting it from the roof."

Emma cleared her throat and spoke just above a whisper. "I knew that he was an alumnus. My father told me. He wouldn't talk a lot about it, but he hinted at some sort of unfortunate incident that happened to him, or because of him, or something like that. That was all that he would say, and I was afraid to bring it up to any of the other professors here. If my father wouldn't talk about it, it was obviously something people didn't want us to know."

Peter sat back in his chair, rubbing his chin. The professor who was an alumnus but didn't want anybody to know, and a rumor that it had something to do with an unfortunate incident. To everyone else, it was curious but not something to lose sleep over, but to Peter, it smelled like a story. He seemed to have gotten lucky with several other stories, including the one he planned to write when they finally caught the dark beings who were trying to take over the school. This could be his next big break.

Izzie looked across the table at Peter and lifted an eyebrow. "I don't know if you should use this one, Peter. I know what you're thinking."

Peter put his hands behind his head and smiled mischievously. "I'm a journalist. I just go where the stories are."

"When we graduated, everything became clear," one of the alumni told a couple of the boys in the boys' dorm after the dinner was over.

Another alumnus chuckled. "You're telling me. I learned so much magic in the first year I was out of high school, it was crazy. I pretty much don't do anything manually in my house because I learned to do it through magic."

One of the boys smiled and looked at the alumni. "Have you learned any magic that helps pick up girls?"

The alumni looked at each other and began to laugh hysterically. "You bet we did. For the longest time, I'm pretty sure the humans who lived near me thought I was a magician. I would go to the barn and pull magic tricks that could be explained away by humans if they thought about it, but it definitely impressed the chicks."

One of the other boys scooted closer. "Would you show us? I mean, you're staying here tonight anyway, and we may or may not see you again, so it's not like you can get in trouble."

One of the alumni laughed. "What are they gonna do to us? Send us to the library for detention?"

Everyone shivered, including the alumni, who were thinking about detention with Librarian Decker. The same alumnus dropped his smile and shook his head. "I spent way too much time with Librarian Decker when I went to the school. I was constantly in detention. He knew me by my first name, and always made sure to give me the hardest tasks."

The boys laughed. "He hasn't changed one bit from the sound of it."

The alumni put their heads together and whispered back and forth, trying to decide what magic trick to do first. Finally, after a few minutes, the first alumnus pulled his wand and leaned in close. "Okay, this is a simple one. At the same time, it's gotten me like a thousand dates."

The boys watched as the alumni swirled his wand over his hand, trying to keep the light as low as possible so he didn't wake any of the other boys. A pink and sparkly string of magic came from the tip of his wand and shimmered into his hand. It created an orb in his palm, and he closed his hand, tapping his wand on his knuckles. He flipped his hand over and opened his palm to reveal a beautiful red rose that bloomed as they watched. One of the boys stuck his hand out and tried to touch it, but when his finger got close, it turned into a magical orb in the shape of a butterfly and flew off.

The alumnus chuckled and shrugged. "Girls like that kind of thing, or at least the human ones do. The magical ones… Well, they're not as easy to impress."

One of the other alums used his elven magic to do another spell. "Getting the chicks is all great, but what you really need to focus on is keeping your life together. Life can get crazy stressful here on Earth. This simple spell will have everything cleaned up for you in a jiffy."

He closed his eyes and whispered an enchantment as he held one hand over the other about six inches apart and turned them counterclockwise in a circle. As he did so, rays of light shone out of them, and an orb popped into his palm. He pulled it up to his mouth and blew on it, watching as it skipped around the room tidying up every space it touched. It only took about three minutes, but by the time it returned to his hand and dissipated into sparks, the entire common area was even tidier than it had been at the beginning of the year.

The boys were impressed. They knew they'd be able to use that one, especially when it came to room inspections. They were about to ask for another one when they heard the footsteps of the proctor coming down the hall. The same alumnus shot out magic, squashing the lights as quickly as he could and then pretending to be asleep.

Connor walked through and checked each room before coming back out and tiptoeing through those who were pretending to sleep on the floor of the common area. He got to his room's threshold and looked back, shaking his head. "Between the squirrels, the kids, and now the alumni…ugh."

The boys' dorm was silent for several moments. All the lights were out, and no one was making a sound. When the light clicked off in the proctor's room and the hallway fell dark, the boy sat up again. One of the students, a Light Elf, flicked his wrist and sent out a small orb of light that bounced across the ceiling lights and turned them on just enough for them to see each other.

One of the alumni nodded. "That was pretty sweet. I didn't learn that until I was in college."

The boy shrugged. "I have three older brothers, and my mom tried to enforce a seven o'clock bedtime when we were kids. It came in really handy."

The guys all chuckled, and the alumnus looked at the students, wondering what else they were capable of. "Why don't you guys show us some spells? Who knows? We may learn something."

One of the boys nodded and pulled out his wand. "I know a trick, something that kept me from getting caught when I snuck out to the orchard with my first girlfriend when I was a sophomore."

The kid stood up and cleared his throat. He closed his eyes and swirled his wand over his head, and shimmering rays of green light whirled around him, then turned to sparks and fell to the floor. As the sparks fell, his body disappeared.

One of the alumni stood up with wide eyes and shook his head. "That's incredible. I'm assuming you are invisible, right?"

"Wrong," the boy said, walking out of the bathroom and brushing the last of the sparks off his robe.

The alumnus laughed, surprised by what the boy had achieved. "Was that a portal?"

The boy nodded. "It was. My dad taught me how to do it when I was younger, and things weren't as peaceful on Earth. He was a Silver Griffin, and had to know how to get out of tight spots quickly while confusing whoever was coming after him. He taught the whole family, just in case someone came after us in our home."

The alumnus chuckled. "I would've used the heck out of that when I was younger. My parents would've never been able to keep me in my room."

The other alumnus looked at him inquisitively. "Did you ever have to use it? When your dad was a Silver Griffin, I mean."

The boy nodded and grew kind of quiet. "Just once, and we all made it out okay. It's a lot more fun when you're trying to escape the professors, though."

The alumnus laughed. "Definitely."

One of the other boys stood up and brushed off his hands. "A squirrel got loose in the dorms last year, or it might have been the year before that; I don't remember.

Either way, it was amazing to watch. One of the proctors almost knocked himself out trying to catch it and, in the end, we ran from it, but it came trotting outside after us. I thought it wise to come up with a magic spell."

One of the alums shook his head. "To catch another squirrel if it happened to get in?"

The boy chuckled and rolled up his sleeves, pulling out his wand. "Not quite."

He swirled his wand, and rays of energy morphed and shifted into the form of a squirrel. At first, it was just light and energy, but as the spell simmered the squirrel sprouted hair. You could actually hear it squeak. It might have been made of magic, but it looked like the real thing.

"I figured it would come in handy if I had to get out of the space quickly and needed a distraction, plus it's hilarious to watch." The boy laughed as the squirrel ran around the room.

He whistled, and the squirrel ran back toward him, leaping through the air and turning back into energy that dissipated back into the tip of the wand. He put the wand in his pocket and took a bow as the boys quietly clapped. He was right, it would definitely get the proctor's attention. Most of the boys hoped he didn't use it anytime soon.

25

The entire campus was quiet. Everyone was either worn out from the dinner party or tired from staying up with some of the alumni and casting spells. The full moon shone brightly, casting a yellow glow over the fields. Through the snores and grumbles of the sleeping students, Luke carefully cracked open his door and edged out, trying desperately not to wake anybody.

He took a step forward, but then jerked back and pressed his back against the doorway. The proctor opened the door down the hall and looked around, but missed Luke standing in the shadows. Luke waited several moments after the proctor shut his door and let out a deep breath, glad that he hadn't gotten caught.

Slowly and carefully he crept barefoot through the common area, weaving between the sleeping students. He looked at them strangely, not sure why they were sleeping out there considering everybody had a room, and so were the alumni. From the looks of it and the cleanliness of the common area, they'd stayed up most the night doing spells.

He chuckled as he stepped over the last kid and hurried down the hallway, trying to step only on the areas of the wooden floor that didn't creak.

When he reached the staircase, he hopped onto the railing and slowly slid down to the bottom. He looked down at the floor, remembering the trick from the game, and touched it with his toe to make sure it was solid. He laughed at himself for being ridiculous and made his way to the front door.

Stepping out into the chilly night air, he took a deep breath and looked up at the bright moon. It was the perfect night to do exactly what he'd dreamt of doing for weeks. Everything had been so crazy at school though, between the Louper matches and the dark magical beings trying to take over, that Luke hadn't had any time for a run.

"Now all I got to do is make it to the spot," Luke whispered.

Luke used his keen sense of hearing and sight to make sure that Horace wasn't out and about on the grounds. The only being he sensed was Dorvu, who was hunting. Luke smiled and took off. He followed the fence all the way to the wooded area, where he disappeared into the trees. His eyes glowed as he ran deeper into the forest until he entered the clearing.

It was lit yellow from the moon, and the leaves on the ground were wilting away into the winter.

"I was starting to wonder if you were going to make it," Henry said, smiling at Luke.

Professor Hodges's eyes were already glowing. "I told you he'd be here. He wouldn't miss out on a run with us tonight. It's too perfect a night, and it's a full moon."

Luke chuckled and walked to the center of the clearing. "I've wanted to do this for weeks now. I was starting to think that I was going to go crazy if I didn't have a chance to."

Professor Hodges nodded and looked at Luke and Henry. "My wolf senses have been on high alert recently, so I want the two of you to be careful while you're out here, just in case something's lurking in the woods. I don't know what's going on. I haven't been able to figure it out yet, but the last thing I want is for the two of you to get hurt while we're running as our wolves. Do you understand?"

Both Luke and Henry nodded. Luke wondered if he was talking about the dark wizards who had been in the forest not long before. He hoped that they weren't out there that night, but at the same time, he kinda hoped they were. He'd love to take a chunk out of one of them.

The professor clapped his hands together and took off his robes. "All right, boys, let's get this going. The wolf in me is dying to come out."

Henry chuckled. "It's better than dying to get back in, that's for sure."

The guys laughed and undressed, leaving their clothes hidden under the shrubbery. They stood in the center of the clearing as their bodies shifted. Hair sprouted on the back of their necks, and they whimpered and howled as they shifted into their wolves. They panted heavily once the shift was complete. The howls of their pack from the surrounding countryside caught their attention. The professor howled back, letting the pack know that they were on the way.

Boys, stay close to me, the professor sent.

With that, they bounded through the woods, the only sound the crunching of the leaves under their paws. It would be a night out for the shifters, and hopefully, nothing but fun. They had seen enough battle and been threatened enough in the last few years. They just wanted to run with their pack and enjoy the few positive things about being a shifter.

Alison was in one of her meditative states when Izzie slipped out of the room, her destination already planned. She snuck down the stairs and out the door and caught a glimpse of Luke disappearing into the woods as she made her way across the fields. She had suspected for a while that Luke did this a lot.

She wasn't as fast as Luke, and the darkness made it hard for her to see. She took her time walking until she reached the edge of the clearing where the moon shone brightly. She peeked through the shrubs as Luke and two other wolves raced off into the woods. She could hear the other members of the pack howling loudly, and it brought a warm sensation to her heart.

Izzie wanted to see more. She wanted to know what they did, and where they went when they were out as their wolves. She stood next to the pile of clothes for a moment and looked around, knowing there was no way she could keep up with them. One thing she *could* do, though, was follow their magical trail. She held her hands out palms-up and pulled the energy from the ground to swirl through her body and warm her.

The symbols on her arms and neck flipped wildly, but she paid them little attention. She didn't realize she had run beyond the edge of the school property and the protection of Professor Powell's spells.

She released an orb that shot into the woods in front of her and picked up the trail of the shifters. Izzie smiled as she moved through trees and around fallen limbs, down gullies and back up again, and kept her eye on the magical trail. She was listening for the sounds of the pack as she walked, and not paying much attention to where she was going.

Just as she was about to take off through a patch of woods, she heard the rustling of leaves to her right and stopped, closing her fist to extinguish the light. She listened closely for a moment and looked around, realizing that she had stumbled onto some sort of camp. To her right was a large tent, tall enough to walk into and not have to bend over. She saw the shadowed silhouettes of the people inside. Izzie knew they weren't students, since camping was not permitted and this was much too far away from the school.

It finally dawned on her. *I'm out here alone, off the campus.*

She inched closer to the tent, looking down at the magical trail that went inside and found nothing but dark magic. Instantly, she knew that those inside the tent weren't friendlies. They were dark wizards.

"The girl is the key. She's not a good key, either. She can bring everything that we've fought for down to rubble," said a wizard.

Izzie listened intently. "She might be able to hide it

from everyone else, but we know what she is and what she can do. She's the only one like her at that school, and this can only go one of three ways. She can be destroyed along with her power, she could turn against us just like that Leira Berens, or we can somehow get her to work with us."

Another wizard spoke up. His voice was dark and deep, and it gave Izzie shivers. "I think the possibilities of her working with us are slim to none, and we know exactly what we need to do. The girl needs to be eliminated before they realize the spells that have been put on them."

"This would be a lot easier if we knew her damn name or even what she looked like," one of the wizards barked. "The headmistress keeps her too close, but our informant said he's seen her walking the grounds at night with another student. Maybe we can lure them outside of the grounds."

Izzie backed away, her breath caught in her throat. She realized very quickly they had to be talking about Alison, or herself. *But why?*

All Izzie could think at that moment was thank goodness they didn't know their names, at least not yet. As she stood there in the trees trying to listen further, her fingers picked at the bracelet on her wrist.

She didn't even realize she was doing it. Izzie pulled off the bracelet, at first surprised at her actions, letting out a small gasp. The energy inside of her sparked, and she felt a soft blow to her solar plexus, throwing her to her knees. She scrambled to her feet and backed up, as the energy built, spreading out to her arms.

Sounds of people talking echoed in her head.

"I love you, my sweet girl," her mother said as memories of her childhood flashed before her eyes.

My mother! Izzie instinctively put up her hands as if she could touch something, swiping her hand through the empty air.

She could hear her mother and father. They were the people she had heard all along. The memories flashed from one to another, rolling through her mind as she clasped a hand over her mouth and watched them flow freely through her. She saw herself dancing with her feet on top of her father's. She saws memories of a childhood filled with love and family. She remembered eating Cheetos with her father, going on runs to a neighborhood store with her mother, and eating dinner with them almost every night.

Who are they?

Izzie strained harder, trying to make out who they were, but she couldn't see their faces. All she could see were flashes of them as they turned to walk away. The memories blew through her so quickly that she struggled to keep her stance. The energy flowed around her wildly, brightening the entire wooded area around her. The dark wizards noticed and walked out of the tent just as the memories faded and the energy flooded back into the bracelet.

Izzie reached down and grabbed it, looking back up at the wizards for a moment before bolting through the woods. The wizards yelled to each other as they chased her, "It's her! Don't let her get through the ward!"

Izzie ran as fast as she could, her skin and eyes still glowing brightly and the symbols on her arms continuing to flip rapidly. She was getting further away from the protective boundary of the school, looking for a way to double back.

As she ran, she slid the bracelet back onto her wrist, feeling the energy immediately subside. It was a strange feeling, something she had never been able to achieve on her own, or at least not that quickly.

Did the headmistress do this on purpose? I don't understand.

Izzie glanced over her shoulder and quickly realized they were gaining on her. There were three of them and only one of her, and they were obviously very in tune with their magic. She leapt over a fallen tree and ran another hundred feet before slowing down and coming to a stop. She clenched her fist and pulled her energy up through her chest, knowing there was no use in running.

She was out there all alone, and she had to fight them.

She ran her fingers over the bracelet as the wizards came to a stop in front of her. Without it, her magic was wild and uncontrollable, but with it, she was limited in what she could do. She didn't know whether to take it off or leave it on to fight them. At first, she felt sorry for herself, that she was all alone without her friends to help her. However, something inside her told her that even though she may not win, she could at least hurt them very badly.

She took a deep breath, and her eyes glowed brighter. She wondered how in the world she knew that. It didn't make any sense, but something in her was not letting go. No matter how weird it was, she just knew she had it in her to do some serious damage to those wizards. She slowly lifted her head and glared at them as they readied their wands, none of them looking confident they could win the fight quickly. They knew what kind of magic she had, but they had no idea what she was capable of.

Izzie steadied herself. If she was going to go down, she would take them with her.

———

Alison ran across the field wearing just her pajamas, using her magic to see the smallest of energies. She clutched the bracelet Shay had given her as she followed Izzie's magical trail into the woods. She knew her friend was in trouble. She had seen it in her meditation, and she couldn't let her fall into the hands of the dark wizards.

She ran as fast as she could manage, slowing down to avoid crashing into the trees, leaves crunching under her bare feet. Her only focus was helping Izzie. As she moved through a clearing, she didn't even pay attention to the shifters' clothes.

She knew she was getting close to Izzie, feeling her magic pulsing through the air.

Alison felt the depth below and hurtled over a gully in a single bound, instinctively using her Drow magic. Her only focus was her friend. Her heart was pounding as she crossed over an open field and through another old growth of trees, acutely aware of the time it was taking to cross the large distance. Her breath caught in her throat as she realized Izzie must have wandered outside the protective ring of spells around the school.

She crested the ridge, and came to a stop, slipping on the bracelet to discern Izzie more easily through the swirl of energy in front of her.

She darted forward and grabbed Izzie by the wrist. "Run!"

Alison threw a blanket of darkness over the area, Izzie held tightly to Alison's wrist as they ran. Alison, able to sense the energy around them, led Izzie out of the complete darkness she had put over the woods.

Izzie tripped, but Alison yanked her back to her feet. "Thanks. This is really bad."

Alison nodded as the darkness began to clear. "You can tell me about it later. Right now, we need to get away."

She looked back as the wizards stumbled through the rapidly dissipating darkness. Alison waved her hands as she twisted the ivy that grew on the forest floor. The wizards burst through the misty darkness, and she threw her hands back, commanding the vines to trip the wizards and hold them down.

"That's new," gasped Izzie.

"Was just pure instinct," said Alison, as she put her hand on her head, grimacing.

Izzie asked, "Are you okay?"

Alison nodded. "I'm going to have to take this bracelet off soon. My head is already starting to kill me."

Izzie was worried about her but didn't know what to say. She shouldn't have been out there all alone at night, but she had found them—the dark wizards who were trying to take down the school. She struggled with the knowledge that she was the girl that they were after. At that point, all she was worried about was making sure that her friend didn't die with her.

26

Dorvu crashed through the canopy, not looking happy at all. The girls ducked as he swooped over their heads and flew toward the wizards. He blew his frosty breath over them, catching one in the leg. She stumbled back, screaming.

Izzie and Alison exchanged looks. Izzie wasn't going to let Dorvu go down like that. "We have to help him. Together we can defeat these guys. I know it's true."

Alison nodded. "I was thinking the same exact thing."

Izzie and Alison immediately took defensive stances. Izzie threw orb after orb of white light straight for the wizard's heads. Alison used a spell they learned in class to distract and created figures all around them with her energy. The wizards were confused long enough for Dorvu to make another pass and slash his claws across one of the wizards' backs.

Izzie continued to throw fireballs at them, even though they were deflected by the wizard's wands. The girls fought hard, and with Dorvu's help, they actually stood a chance. It was a longshot, though. The wizards were obviously very talented and very strong.

Alison gritted her teeth and narrowed her eyes as one of the wizards sent a stream of magic at Dorvu and knocked him into the woods. Her eyes glowed black as her magic crawled along the forest floor like vines. "You do not hurt one of our own!"

One of the wizards chuckled and shot a fireball at Alison, but when it got close, she raised her hand and stopped it in its tracks. She cocked her head and examined it as it hovered before her, then wrapped her hand around it and crushed it in her palm. The wizard backed up, slightly taken aback by her powers.

Suddenly Horace's dog raced past Alison and Izzie and leapt through the air, sinking its teeth into one of the wizards and taking him down to the ground. Horace jogged up to the girls and nodded. "Don't you figure you're out of bed a little bit late?"

Izzie chuckled and shook her head. "I think we have more to worry about right now than my bedtime."

Horace shrugged. "I don't know. Seems as if you've got everything under control here, so…"

Alison laughed. From her left, Headmistress Berens blasted through the trees using her elven powers. At first, both the girls wanted to draw back, realizing that they were going to be in trouble, but as the headmistress began to fight the wizards, they knew they couldn't leave her on her own. Besides, it wasn't like she didn't know they were there.

Alison grabbed Izzie by the wrist and nodded toward the fight. "Come on! We need to back her up!"

Izzie looked at the sky and smiled. "I think Dorvu might have that under control."

Everyone ducked as Dorvu crashed through the trees and grabbed two of the wizards by their shoulders with his long claws. They screamed and dropped their wands as Dorvu carried them off. Everyone stood still for a moment watching as Dorvu got smaller on the horizon. He finally stopped and hovered, then dropped both wizards from the sky.

Izzie's eyes grew wide, and she looked at Horace, who nodded, impressed. "He's pretty tough. Tougher than I thought he was going to be."

The last wizard ran for the woods. The headmistress let him go, knowing that the dark families needed to receive the message not to mess with them. The headmistress stomped toward them and shook her finger in Izzie's face angrily. "What in the hell is going on? What are you doing out here? Who were they?"

Izzie just looked at her, a mixture of fear and anger boiling inside her. She knew now that the headmistress had something to do with her not knowing who her family was, but now that she had seen her mother and father and knew she wasn't an orphan, things had changed. Izzie was reluctant to say anything to the headmistress, not wanting to give away what she had seen or that she had gone to find Luke.

The headmistress turned to Alison and narrowed her eyes. "Well, Alison? What is going on here?"

Alison looked at her, then at Izzie. She did not want to get Izzie in trouble or spill secrets that weren't hers to tell. The headmistress got angrier and angrier as she waited for answers. Finally, as she was about to turn back to Izzie, Alison spoke.

"Okay. Izzie and I came out for a walk after curfew. Since I meditate and don't sleep, and since Izzie doesn't sleep very much because of her dreams, walking the grounds helps us work through our problems and calm down at night. Anyway, we were out walking and talking. We weren't paying attention to where we were going, and we ran into the bad guys—the dark wizards."

The headmistress pressed her lips together, angry. "They are getting more and more aggressive."

Izzie shrugged. "They are determined."

The headmistress clapped her hands together. "Horace, call an emergency late-night meeting immediately."

"What in the world is going on?" asked Professor Hudson, standing with her robe clutched around her.

Professor Regency climbed up into one of the chairs so he could face everyone. "Whatever it is, it can't be good."

Professor Fowler spoke up. "The dark wizards were right outside the school grounds, camping in the woods. Izzie and Alison were out after curfew and walked up on them."

The crowd of teachers standing in the conference room gasped. None of them had had any idea that the dark wizards were that close, or that they were planning anything.

"Are the girls okay?" one of the teachers asked.

"Yes, they are okay. They fought valiantly until the headmistress showed up," Professor Fowler reported as she scrunched her hair and held her robe closed around her.

Professor Regency gritted his teeth. "We need to go look for them. We can't let them get away with this. It's obvious they're part of a dark family. A message needs to be sent out immediately."

One of the teachers crossed her arms over her chest. "Is it even safe to have the students here?"

Professor Fowler held up her hand as the teachers began to talk louder. "We don't even know the full extent of what is going on yet. There is no use panicking them at this point. The last thing we need right now is more chaos. It's too soon to discuss sending the students home. We need to fully understand what we're facing, and the only person who can explain that to us is the headmistress."

Just then the headmistress walked in, silencing them all. "The problem is insidious. The dark wizards and witches have stepped up their game of trying to take down the school. It is essential that we provide the best protection to the school and the students, so we are going to implement night patrols immediately. Also, Leo Decker is looking into better wards for us. It's obvious that the ones we have aren't helping very much."

Headmistress Berens turned to Professor Powell and nodded. "Going to need your help on this."

Professor Powell nodded. "Of course."

"I don't know how safe it is to ask the teacher of dark

magic to help you combat dark magic," one of the teachers shouted.

Professor Powell whipped around, staring at the teacher. "Who better to counter darkness than someone who understands it?"

27

Izzie and Alison were still shaken from the fight but made it to the Louper game a few days later. The stands were full of students cheering wildly for their team. Izzie gripped the rail, looking out over the field where Luke stood, preparing for the game. For her, everything looked different. Everything *was* different. It was almost like she was seeing the world through different eyes.

"Welcome to today's SNM Cardinals Louper match. They will be competing for the regional title!" the headmistress called from where she was standing on the field.

Everyone cheered loudly, waving their flags high in the air as the wind whipped across the field. It was cold out, but no one seemed to notice. They were all too excited to see their team go on after five straight wins. The headmistress smiled and waited for everyone to settle down a bit.

"Our Cardinals will be playing the Coyotes!"

The crowd booed, but the headmistress held up her hand, wrinkling her nose. She was all about good sportsmanship, even if the other team wasn't present to hear the crowd booing. She wanted to keep it upbeat and happy. She turned toward the team and nodded. "Good luck today, Cardinals. I'll be watching from the stands. No matter what the outcome is, you have played an amazing season so far."

Henry looked at Wyatt as they stood on the sidelines waiting for everything to begin. "Did the coach tell you what our scenario will be?"

Wyatt whispered to Henry. "You know that's not allowed…but yes. We'll be in a dense forest on Oriceran. I'm just hoping the newbies don't go all tourist on me like they did last time. We need to win this game. I am *not* going to let the Coyotes beat us again."

Henry nodded. "You're damn right. They may think they have one up on us because they can come into our scenarios, but we're ready for them this time. We learned our lesson, and I'm not going to lose regionals."

Wyatt looked down the line and chuckled. "From the looks of the other guys, they're not going to let them go either. Apparently, that game was heard round the world. Even the freshmen knew about it before they entered the school. There's a rivalry on top of a rivalry going on here. We've got something to prove, and the Coyotes are too cocky to even think we would remember. I can promise you, when we get into those woods on Oriceran, every-one's head is going to be in the game."

Henry clapped as the referee walked out onto the field. "Good, because I'm ready to kick some ass."

The referee read the rules and allowed the Coyotes a few moments on their field before they disappeared into their side of the scenario. He raised his wand and sent a green shower of sparks over the players. They all closed their eyes and clenched their fists, waiting for the virtual playing field to rise in front of them.

Just as Wyatt had suspected, when he opened his eyes, none of the players on his team were even *close* to being in tourist mode. Everyone was focused and ready to go. Wyatt gathered them in a circle and put his arms over Henry's and Luke's shoulders. "This team likes to play games, as you all know from last year. Keep your eyes open, and don't be afraid to strike whenever you see something that doesn't look remotely okay. We're in the forest of Oriceran and there a lot of things out there that'll get you, but the Coyotes—they won't stop. Luke, Henry, and I will be heading up the three teams. Let's get this going and take ourselves to the finals."

Everyone put their hands into the center and yelled their battle cry before splitting up into their three groups. Luke led his team through the woods and into a small clearing, where he knelt to go over strategy.

Luke looked at each of the boys and nodded. "This is our chance. We're not missing this one. I want us to head east through the woods and toward the cliffs. Keep your eyes open, and your magic at the ready. When we get to the cliffs, don't make the same mistakes we made last year. Keep an eye out for dragons and harpies that like to grab you and throw you over the edge. We're a team. We win as a team, or we fail as a team. Let's win."

Everybody nodded, and they crept through the outskirts of the woods. They could hear all kinds of sounds coming through the forest. Most sounded like large birds or ferocious lions. As they approached the tree line that opened onto the grassy field skirting the edges of the cliffs, they crouched in the bushes and looked out.

"I can see the treasure across the cliffs. I say we make a run for it. Have your weapons ready and your magic at hand," Luke told the team.

As they stepped into the field, dragons descended and picked up several of the boys, dropping them over the cliffs. Luke bent down and looked at one of his wizard teammates. "You think maybe you could make me a weapon with that wand?"

Luke was just kidding, but the boy twisted his wand, and out shot a stream of light that quickly turned into a long sword. He handed the sword to Luke, who lifted his eyebrows. "That'll do."

Luke stood up and swung the sword at the dragons overhead. They swooped down but retreated as the blade struck their scales. The other boys used their magic, shooting streams of light at the dragons. Several of them hit the dragons' wings and sent them toppling over the cliffs. Luke used his shifter strength to wield the heavy sword, and the magic spread across the dragon as he struck.

They fought hard and long, beating the dragons back until finally the beasts retreated into the distance. Luke stood on the edge of the cliffs trying to catch his breath as he turned back to the other guys. They were down quite a few, but a few were still standing, and that was all that mattered. From the woods, the sound of rustling leaves and crunching twigs caught his attention.

He held his sword out in front of him and narrowed his eyes. "Who's there?"

Henry, Wyatt, and their teams stepped out, clapping. Henry chuckled and shook his head. "That was pretty impressive. I won't lie."

Luke let out a sigh and dropped his sword to the side. "You guys are still alive."

Wyatt shrugged. "For now…"

Just then a stream of light shot from the trees above them and morphed into dozens of dark arrows. Luke watched in horror as two of the arrows struck Wyatt and Henry in their chests, forcing them out of the game. Their team was going down quickly. Luke snapped his head up and saw a member of the Coyotes perched in the treetops, firing magical arrows at his teammates.

His eyes grew bright yellow, and he growled as he ran for the tree and used his shifter muscles to leap onto a branch. The Coyote's eyes grew wide, and he threw fireballs rapidly at Luke. What he hadn't expected was for Luke to have a weapon—a magical one—that he used to smack the fireballs back into the forest.

Luke looked down at his sword and sighed. "It'd be really nice if this was a lot shorter."

The sword sparkled and shifted from a long sword into a dagger. Luke looked at it in surprise, then shrugged. "That'll do."

He threw the dagger as hard as he could at the Coyote player, and it soared through his chest, causing him to disappear out of the game. Luke nodded and jumped down, landing in front of what remained of his team. He looked at them, then across the cliffs to where the treasure sat sparkling in the Oriceran sun.

Luke was sore and worn down, but it was only this group left, and they had to get there before the other team did. "I'm not taking any chances. You guys stay here. Keep an eye out for more Coyotes, and don't let the dragons get you. Hopefully, I'll be done before anything like that happens."

The team looked at him curiously as he walked to the edge of the cliff, rolling his shoulders. He allowed part of his wolf to take over. Long claws grew from his hands, and his muscles twitched and hardened as he slowly backed up and made a running leap off the cliff. He soared through the air as the dragons descended, trying to attack him as he flew toward the treasure.

Mid-air, he slashed his claws at the dragons, digging deep beneath their scales and sending them plummeting into the water below. He tilted his body back until his feet were downward and landed right in front of the treasure, and looked back at the cheering team and beamed as he grabbed it. The scenario ended, and he found himself holding the treasure in the middle of the field. His team members and he were all back on the playing fields, with no Coyotes around.

The stadium's silence held for just a moment before the spectators went wild, screaming Luke's name and running onto the field. His team plowed into him, jumping up and down and holding the treasure high in the air. All the exhaustion and soreness Luke had felt at the end of the game quickly faded away, at least for the moment.

"I knew you could do it," Izzie said, as she wrapped her arms around his waist.

Luke smiled and kissed Izzie. "You're always my inspiration."

Izzie smiled and backed off as the team lifted Luke onto their shoulders. He held the treasure high in the air, and the crowd went wild once again, waving their flags and celebrating to the accompaniment of victory music in the background. The team led the way, carrying Luke off the field and heading to the dining hall to celebrate winning the first semester tournament. It was going to be one of the largest celebrations since he'd started playing Louper, and although it wasn't his first win, it felt like the best ever. "On to the next tournament," he shouted.

Izzie grabbed Alison by the hand, and they walked behind the crowd caught up in the celebration. "I guess that didn't turn out so badly after all."

Alison squeezed her hand. "We'll make sure that nothing turns out badly, even if we have to fight for it."

"Professor Fowler, do you want to make a statement about the emergency meeting called for the teachers the other night?" Peter asked, shadowing Professor Fowler around the school.

The professor turned to Peter and narrowed her eyes. "How do you know about that?"

Peter shrugged "I'm a good journalist and I have my sources."

Professor Fowler looked at him for another minute and shook her head. "I don't have anything to say about it, and if I were you, I would back off. The headmistress won't be happy that you're trying to print this in the newspaper."

Peter backed up and let Professor Fowler walk away, shaken. He shadowed teachers all day long, trying to get someone to tell him what had happened the other night. Truth was, he was his own source.

He hadn't been able to sleep and was downstairs getting a snack from the cafeteria when the emergency meeting was called, and the headmistress came stomping through the entryway.

Izzie stopped next to Peter and lifted an eyebrow. "Professor Fowler just pushed past me. I've never seen her look like that. What in the world did you do to her?"

Peter shook his head. "I didn't do anything. I asked about the emergency meeting the other night."

Izzie immediately clammed up, pulling away, but Peter grabbed her arm. "You *do* know something about it. I thought I saw you and Alison out there, but I figured it was just because I was tired. I didn't think you two would actually go out by yourselves late at night with the dark wizards nearby."

Alison walked up next to Izzie. "He knows, doesn't he?"

Izzie sighed and hung her head. "I think he's put it together."

Peter pulled them both to the side. "You have to tell me what's going on if you know something about the dark families."

Izzie held up a placating hand. "Okay, I was out there tracking Luke the other night, and I found the dark wizards' camp. They were talking about the student they were trying to find, and I realized that it just might be me. They saw my magic and chased me down, and that's when Alison showed up."

Alison nodded. "I was meditating, and I saw it, so I ran after Izzie. Along with Dorvu, Horace, his dog, and the headmistress, we fought them off. One got away, and Dorvu carried the other two off."

Peter wrinkled his forehead and bit the inside of his lip. "I just don't get it. It doesn't fit together anymore, not that it ever did. Why are they searching for this student—or you, Izzie, if it is you? What does some young magical have to do with them taking over the school?"

"Maybe it's not me." Izzie gave a shrug. What would all of her memories have to do with the dark families? It didn't make sense to her.

"Maybe it's me," said Alison. "My father worries about this kind of thing. That's why he's making sure I'm well trained."

Izzie took a deep breath and shook her head. "I think they have someone on the inside, Peter, who's helping them and whatever it is they're planning we need to find out."

"What are you all doing?" asked Jason, striding up confidently. He always seemed to turn up at the wrong moment. Everyone grew silent as Peter quickly changed the subject.

"Making plans to get to every Louper game next semester."

Jason narrowed his eyes but the smile stayed frozen on his face.

The headmistress stood at her office window and stared at Izzie as she walked across the courtyard with Alison and the others. She sent out an invisible streak of energy that lit Izzie's magical signature. It was changing with every memory Izzie pulled from her past.

The headmistress sighed, stepped away from the window, and sat down at her desk, clutching her hands in front of her. She knew that her spell wasn't going to hold much longer, if it was even still holding at all.

I thought Izzie would come to me if she remembered. But after seeing the look on Izzie's face the other night in the woods, she knew there was more to it than what Izzie was saying.

Jasper Elf magic was powerful, and when mixed with that of the silver dragon, it was almost unstoppable. Things were falling apart quickly, and the headmistress hadn't even had the time to wrap her head around it before the dark wizards had shown up on Izzie's tail. It could've been much worse, but luckily Izzie's magical signature had been close enough that the headmistress was able to follow it into the woods. She knew that if it had been only two more weeks later, she might not have been able to pick it up.

Headmistress Berens sighed again and walked over to the shelf, pulling the box down. She set it on a small table and tapped it with her wand, listening to the lock click. Slowly, she opened the lid and looked down at the balls, which were almost completely covered by dark shadows. They were deteriorating at an accelerated pace.

The headmistress closed the box with frustration and returned it to the shelf, walking back over to the window and watching as Izzie and Alison disappeared into the barn. She didn't know what Alison's role was going to be in all of it, but it was obvious that wherever Izzie was, so was Alison. She was starting to think it wasn't such a bad thing, considering Alison had such strong powers. Her real concerns were far from that, though.

She rubbed her hands down her face and let out a deep breath. She had made Izzie's parents a promise, but she was struggling to keep it. She'd had no idea when she made that vow that things would turn out the way that they had. But with the way that the balls were deteriorating, she knew there was more to it than just Izzie's memory.

Does that mean the parents are starting to remember too?

Jason Patrick waited till dark before he set out for the kemana. He was careful to make sure no one was following him. He couldn't risk being spotted, there was too much at stake. He was headed to a meeting and he knew full well that the others didn't take failure very well.

He chewed on his bottom lip nervously as he opened the door to the kemana and made his way down the wide steps, stepping into the light from the glowing rock in the center.

He made his way quickly to the pub, his collar turned up by his face, his shoulders hunched and walked in past a Kilomea who glanced down and grunted at him.

Jason shook just a little from fear but didn't look up.

"You're late," grumbled one of the wizards.

"Shut up, Clancy, at least you got your warm beer and we're not in the woods."

"I said beer and warm seat."

"You have it?"

The two dark wizards looked anxiously at Jason.

"Yeah, I have it." He hesitated, wondering if he should do it as he pulled out his phone and showed them a picture of Izzie and Alison. "Is this who you mean?"

"Yeah, that's her. Tell us all about her. You've done well, kid. Your dad will be proud."

Jason reluctantly smiled. It was all he ever wanted.

"I don't have much time. I have to get back before I'm missed or worse, someone sees me."

"Then hurry, and we'll take it from there."

The snow was falling heavily in Charlottesville as the students made their way from the bus to the Starbucks at the start of their Christmas break. Alison, Izzie, and the group rode together, loaded down with gifts that they'd exchanged before they left the mansion. Luke had gotten Izzie a beautiful snowflake ring, and she'd quickly put it on her finger and kissed him. She was going to miss him during Christmas break, but at least she had that to keep him in her mind.

Tanner had gotten Alison a charm bracelet and a charm with both their names written in braille. She'd smiled, put it on her wrist, and kissed him on the cheek. It was the perfect gift. She could wear it around Brownstone, and he would never know what it said.

As they walked through the Starbucks, they talked happily about their Christmas vacations. Tanner had his arm around Alison, with Jason in the background watching with envy. Luke and Izzie held hands, lost in a kind of love haze as they made their way through the magical wall of the Starbucks and into the train station.

"Remind me again where you're going for Christmas break?" Luke asked Izzie.

Izzie giggled and held onto the railing as they made their way down to the platform. "I'm going to LA with Alison to celebrate Christmas with Brownstone and Shay. They were so kind to me when they came last year for the dance. They invited me, and surprisingly, the headmistress said it was okay."

Luke looked at her nervously, knowing only part of what had happened at the woods that night. "And you're sure you'll be safe?"

Alison walked up beside them and put her arm around Luke's shoulders. "Are you serious? I'm pretty sure that in a house with Shay and Brownstone, not to mention her own badass abilities, she's in the safest place she could possibly be."

Izzie clapped her hands in excitement. "And I'll be with my best friend."

Alison reached out and squeezed Izzie's hand. "We could even go out on a bounty hunt together."

Izzie's mouth dropped open in excitement. "Another adventure. Maybe even a career."

Luke put up his finger and shook his head. "I don't really like the idea of that. Can't you two just, I don't know, do human girl things?"

Izzie laughed. "And what exactly are human girl things?"

Luke shrugged. "I don't know. Painting your toenails?"

Tanner jumped in. "Gossiping? Going to the salon?"

Ethan laughed and stuck his head between the two groups. "I think you boys are digging yourself a hole."

Kathleen rolled her eyes, waiting for everyone on the center platform. "I think you're probably an expert at that by now."

Everybody laughed and made their way down to Kathleen. Izzie felt the tightness in her chest, and a partial memory broke through. It was her mother saying something about going on a bounty hunt.

The voice of her mother echoed through her mind. "We won't be long, and you know how to use spells."

Luke draped his arm around Izzie and kissed her on the forehead, pulling her from her memory. "You okay?"

Izzie shook it off and smiled. "Yeah. I just got entranced by the thought of Christmas with Alison, that's all."

Izzie took a deep breath and stored that memory in the back of her mind, knowing it was something she could investigate when she got back. As much as she wanted to think about all the memories she had just received, she also wanted to enjoy her Christmas break. She didn't want to get stuck in the past and miss everything in the present.

Emma opened her arms and hugged each of the people in the group. "I go off to the right. My train's down there a bit. Everyone have a very Merry Christmas, and please, please be safe."

One by one, the group said their goodbyes and headed in different directions. Izzie and Alison stood at the platform waving goodbye to Tanner, Luke, and the others as they disappeared into the different tunnels to make their way to their platforms.

Alison took Izzie's hand and smiled. "Merry Christmas, Izzie."

Izzie squeezed Alison's hand and looked down as the train pulled into the station. "Merry Christmas, Alison. This is going to be the best Christmas ever!"

Alison is heading into her Junior Year of high school. For most of us that's when things get a little easier. We can drive, we're not the newbies, and we're still a year away from the pressure of getting into college. (Yeah, I know that pressure starts early)

But it's also a mixed bag of trying to figure out who we are and how we fit into the world as compared to our peers and to the world out there.

I was a tall string bean with wild curly hair before the invention of hair products who always thought she was too fat. But, there's a little wisdom in there for me to root out if I want to and learn something from looking back at the younger days and reading (or writing) about teenage struggles.

I can change the way I look at not only my past, but the day I'm in right now. I can look back and see how beautiful that creature was and how curious about the world. How brave she was too. I volunteered to be in a debate about women's rights in front of a crowd from an all-male boarding school. The opposing view was that the woman should stay home because 'it comes out of her'. This was 1976 by the way. I held my own despite the fact the audience nodded their heads in agreement with him.

I was often the odd opinion in my crowd and it was going to be a while before I learned – I wasn't wrong, just different and needed to move along to a different place.

I was an odd girl out for other reasons too. My dad, always thinking, was able to find a grant for female descendants of Civil War soldiers who lost their land in the war. Coupled with the discount because he was an Episcopal minister, I found myself at a private girls' school. It exposed me to great culture and life -long friends, *and* pointed out more than once how poor we really were.

We went to a play at the Kennedy Center with the local private boys' school and I had a dress for the occasion but not the appropriate shoes and wore my loafers – the best I had. There was a lot of snickering and finger pointing at the bus. I did my best to act like I didn't see it three feet away.

Mix in that I had opinions of my own and already wanted to set out into the world and be a journalist and writer, and a wife and mother. I got laughed at a lot but fortunately, not be everybody. There were also adults who saw my potential and encouraged me. Every chance I get I try to do the same and pay it forward. The world is better off with everyone contributing what makes them unique.

Here's what I will say to that younger version of myself and it's the same thing I want the present me to know – and act on (where the real power is because I can still do something about today) –

You have something unique to offer the world. Go find the crowd that supports your ideas, celebrates them and adds to them. Do the same for them. Move away from those who are looking for the problem and join in with those working for a solution. Try your ideas and when you hit a wall, look at the data, ask for help from positive and appropriate sources and keep going. Be kind and compassionate, give people the benefit of the doubt, be willing to walk away when it's not working and do that with compassion too, stay flexible and willing, say less and listen more, explore your creativity to their limits and then reach further, trust that things are always working out the way they're supposed to, and make sure you're having a lot of fun doing it.

More adventures to follow.

THANK YOU for not only reading this story but these *Author Notes* as well!

I finally get to talk about Alison Anderson becoming Alison Brownstone! The most recent release of *The Unbelievable Mr. Brownstone* just came out, and it is interesting what some of the readers are chatting about. With that series focused more on adults than this one, I often get a bunch of fans who chant, "Fight fight fight!" But I didn't want to make that book all about fighting.

Exactly.

No, it was supposed to become the first book of what causes Alison to get a certain harder edge. We are going to be seeing just how much more by Book 08 (the end of this series), and then Alison's personal series after this one.

TUMB09 was also about Alison's desire to remain James' daughter. Family, as she says in the story, isn't always about blood.

Here we show that Alison has more on her mind than

just school and that the ties to those that she holds dear are stronger than blood.

Beijing, China

Right now, I'm typing this while sitting on the bullet train between Beijing and Shanghai, China. In the distance, past the large fields of green (and trees) are tall buildings hosting many families. Or, they might be empty, I can't tell at this distance.

Our days in Beijing were fun and focused on the 2018 Beijing Book Fair. It was supposed to be a vacation type for me, and work for Judith (who has responsibility for foreign rights.) It turned out I was at the fair a lot more than I had figured I would be. On the plus side, it was very interesting and provided me with an opportunity to engage with a fantastic interactive display that focused on their language.

Now, I'm easily overwhelmed by languages. I don't understand the phonetic differences many times, and Japanese and Chinese glyphs scare the crap out of me. Trying to learn it (I thought) would be a monumental task, and why the hell start? I'm fifty. It's not like I am a young puppy. (Editor's note: He's just a lad. I tell him so all the time.)

However, from that short experience, I'm curious about the characters and what they mean.

For me to even make it this far, I had to learn to get over my hesitation at trying new experiences and just start walking in and out of the different areas with Judith. There is nothing like going into a vast hall where you can't read much of anything—and certainly don't speak the language—and just pointing.

The people at the Fair, and frankly almost ALL the people we met, were friendly and patient with two Americans who didn't speak but two words of Chinese.

"Hello" and *"Thank You."*

So, "Thank you, Beijing" for welcoming us as we visited your city.

And THANK YOU for choosing Coke over Pepsi. (Except Pizza Hut, you <redacted>.) I was able to drink as much of the elixir of wakefulness as I desired.

Ad Aeternitatem,

Michael Anderle

- Rule of Magic (4) - Dealing in Magic (5) - Theft of Magic (6) -
Enemies of Magic (7) - Guardians of Magic (8)

The Soul Stone Mage Series

* Sarah Noffke and Martha Carr *

House of Enchanted (1) - The Dark Forest (2) - Mountain of
Truth (3) - Land of Terran (4) - New Egypt (5) - Lancothy (6) -
Virgo (7)

The Kacy Chronicles

* A.L. Knorr and Martha Carr *

Descendant (1) - Ascendant (2) - Combatant (3) - Transcendent
(4)

The Midwest Magic Chronicles

* Flint Maxwell and Martha Carr*

The Midwest Witch (1) - The Midwest Wanderer (2) - The
Midwest Whisperer (3) - The Midwest War (4)

The Fairhaven Chronicles

* with S.M. Boyce *

Glow (1) - Shimmer (2) - Ember (3) - Nightfall (4)

www.ingramcontent.com/pod-product-compliance
Lightning Source LLC
Chambersburg PA
CBHW050244110726

47898CB00007B/2270